Praise for Becoming Marta

"One of the best books of 2011. Tremendously entertaining, this novel captivates from the first line to the last; the happy discovery of an authentic writer . . . [Becoming Marta] expands upon the idea of literary entertainment."

—Sergio González Rodríguez, *El Ángel* magazine

"Great book! I read it in one sitting. I love the clean prose, so seemingly simple yet hiding many hours of intense work."

—Juan Luis Cebrián, author of *Red Doll* and other novels, CEO of PRISA, journalist, novelist, and member of the Royal Spanish Academy

"[Lorea Canales offers a] female voice who seeks her identity, exposes her distress, and shows her power through a character who thinks and acts within the realm of social privilege. It is this wealthy family that the novel deconstructs, showing its flaws and tics, the way people present themselves to the outside world and the conflicts that destroy them from the inside. Canales makes a bold and assured debut, with effective use of dialogue, contributing stories that will form the future."

—Diamela Eltit, author of *E. Luminata* and other novels, winner of the José Donoso Prize for lifetime achievement

"[Becoming Marta is] well worth reading. I felt trapped. Lorea Canales has the talent to invent three-dimensional characters who become flesh and blood. The reader ends up believing in them. They are fictional characters so well crafted that each has a unique voice."

—José Manuel Prieto, author of *Encyclopedia of a Life in Russia* and *Rex: A Novel*

"With rare subtlety, Lorea Canales's debut novel connects the current Mexican narrative with great literature."

—Mario Bellatín, author of *Beauty Salon* and other novels

"An intelligent and enjoyable novel."

—*Voy y Vengo* magazine

"The start of a great literary career. [Lorea Canales] finds a way to enter many worlds. Canales engages in psychological explorations. She is a humanist, searching to comprehend the environment, to understand the world."

—Jesús Silva Herzog-Márquez, author of *La idiotez de lo perfecto* and other essays, columnist for *Reforma* newspaper

"Lorea Canales succeeds with her first novel. Marta has all the makings of a universally loved soap opera character, but readers of *Becoming Marta* will discover someone much more complex: a protagonist who is emblematic of a new generation of young urban adults in Latin America and the United States."

—Arturo Conde, Univision News

Becoming Marta

Lorea Canales

Becoming Marta

TRANSLATED BY GABRIEL AMOR

amazon crossing

Previously published as *Apenas Marta* in Mexico in 2011 by Plaza Janes. Translated from Spanish by Gabriel Amor. First published in English by AmazonCrossing in 2016.

Published by AmazonCrossing, Seattle

www.apub.com

Amazon, the Amazon logo, and AmazonCrossing are trademarks of Amazon.com, Inc., or its affiliates.

ISBN-13: 9781503952614

ISBN-10: 1503952614

Cover design by David Drummond

Printed in the United States of America

For Ana and Julia in their becoming

Spring Blossom

Ser
Devenir
Become
What kind of woman
are you?
What will you be when you grow up?
Wait . . . aren't you already?
Yes, yes . . . I am
and yet
I do not know
what I will become.
Do flowers find becoming hard
or do they bloom effortlessly?
Maybe I already bloomed,
it was a great day.
The problem, then, consists in decay
or is it decaying?

1

The House

It is not easy to enter a party. The heat outside was deadly; the sun had set, darkness settled, but the heat remained. Marta climbed the stairs to the main *palapa*. She stood watching, her hair wet and feet bare, the straps of her sandals held by two fingers of her left hand. The guests had already gathered; all but three of them were familiar. She sat down on the limestone steps, put on her heels, and walked toward the grand *palapa*, where they were mingling. She scanned the strangers invited by Gaby, her father's new wife. She took in their stares, transforming them into a loathing that she exhaled like cigarette smoke.

She stopped in front of the pool, which was shining in the dark night, aware that the light passing between her legs made her silhouette visible to everyone. Most of them had already seen her in a bikini— some had even seen her naked—so what did it matter? Her mother would've said, "Close your legs, move out of the light, sit properly."

"Bring me a Paloma Blanca," she said to the air, certain that a waiter would hear her. Sure enough, a glass of white tequila and Sprite was placed in her hand. She pursed her lips against the ice-filled glass as memories filled her. She gulped down the drink to quiet her thirst and the heat. The silk clung to her body.

Marta turned to the guests. There was Juan Estrada. She remembered the last time she'd been with him. He'd called her when his wife had gone to Valle de Bravo. They'd gone out to dinner and then back to his place. He'd started kissing her, undressing her; suddenly, he'd stopped, sat on the bed with his underwear between his knees, covered his face, and started crying. The pathetic reality of having his impotence exposed had turned into fury. "Get out!" he'd screamed at her in a hoarse voice that seemed to rise from the depths of his gut. "Don't you see? There's nothing to be done here."

Marta had considered holding him, getting closer. After all, that's why she'd gone home with him—for a fleeting moment of comfort, a moment of feeling cared for or maybe even loved. But Marta had managed to control this impulse. She grabbed her things and slammed the door on the way out. *You're pathetic,* she thought, uncertain if she was referring to him or to herself.

Marta took another sip of her drink. The sea and sky, everything was black—a funereal darkness. A cliff above the sea, a hill above the cliff, and a house above the hill. To build the house, they'd had to destroy the hill. Trees and tons of red clay were removed, rearranged, and flattened. One night a powerful storm washed half the hillside into the sea. For days a huge brown stain was visible below the cliff. The contractor took note of this process, calculating costs and savings. From then on, instead of carting the dirt miles away, he dumped it in the ocean.

The architect was all too familiar with his clients' contradictions. They wanted an extraordinary house, something palatial with no expense spared. But they also sought simplicity and discretion. This was not the time for ostentation. For that reason he'd concealed the house behind leafy gardens with fully grown trees transplanted from what little jungle remained. He also planted many palm tree saplings, knowing that everything sprouted and grew quickly here. At first the royal palms that bordered the driveway had barely been three feet tall. Now they were tall and wide, leafy with smooth, elegant trunks.

Marta recalled a time when she still liked the house and praised its virtues. She had even been proud of it. It had featured prominently on the cover of a coffee-table book about beach houses. Now it weighed on her. Seeing her father and Gaby there disgusted her. It made her ill to think that they slept on the same sheets her mother had bought, that they used the same dishes. The house had to go.

2
The Mother

Marta's image of her mother before they operated on her: an eggshell underneath a threadbare cotton robe; a green, faded robe that provided no comfort; her mother anesthetized, distant. Was it really her or just her body? Where was her mother behind that veil of medications? Somewhere else—she was already somewhere else.

The scars on her breasts and, after he'd mutilated her, the doctor's verdict: "There is nothing to be done; it has spread." The amputation was useless, too late.

"Do you remember Saint Agatha? She didn't have anesthesia," her mother had said, still holding on to her sense of humor.

Paintings of the saint and martyr with her breasts on a silver tray immortalized in the galleries of the Uffizi and the Prado: obligatory sights on European tours that had made such an impression on Marta as a child and whose happy memories had faded. There remained only the image of her mother's severed breasts, full of blood and displayed like objects, as though they'd never belonged to a body. They resembled mountains more than flesh, or clay mounds like the volcanoes children make in science class that erupt by mixing vinegar and baking soda.

Then there was her father's stupidity. Ignoring both Marta's and her mother's wishes, and taking advantage of their momentary weakness, he had decided that she should remain in Houston. He'd left his wife in the hospital to endure treatments—more torture, more senselessness, more suffering—rather than letting her come home where she belonged, and where Marta could have employed several English ladies experienced with hospice care, who managed the process of dying by administering doses of morphine. But no. Instead of linen sheets and pale-peach curtains that filtered sunlight on the vase always filled with white roses, instead of the fine nightdress and cashmere robe—vain comforts, but comforts nonetheless—there was the inhospitable hospital, loathsome in its fake cheeriness and the nurses' bad manners. The scrawny robe and the experimental treatments were nothing more than absurd, costly torture. Then there was death. Marta was left hanging, waiting for a final conversation with her mom. Waiting to discuss things they'd never discussed. Was it true what they said? Was it true? But her mother was not there to answer.

She was a corpse that needed to be repatriated. She was a process the imbecile consul had not expedited. He was an inexperienced bureaucrat from the new administration, lacking any concept of class, who sought to democratize her mother's corpse. The corpse of Señora Tordella de la Vega, whose surname all of Mexico recognized. The imbecile tried to treat it like the corpse of any old immigrant. They said he resigned when his boss, alerted from Mexico, ordered the consul to provide the corpse with special treatment. "The bastard turned out to have integrity," her father had said.

In the end, and despite the family's official silence on the matter, the gossip magazines covered the funeral. People attended in order to see and be seen, to make others believe that they were part, or had been part, of her mother's life. "Poor Marti. She was always so cheerful . . .

It came on so suddenly . . . What a shock. Oh! You never know, it hits when you least expect it . . . We're so sorry . . . You can't know how much I loved your mother . . . My most sincere condolences." Empty phrases repeated ad infinitum. The cards, flowers, and even framed photographs that arrived at the house with ridiculous notes: "I found this picture of your mother. It's a fantastic photo and I thought you'd like to have it." *Do they think we don't have our own photographs?*

3

The Search

"Take me to see her," said Marta, getting in the car after her dance class.

After school Marta's chauffeur—sometimes still accompanied by a nanny, depending on the day of the week—took her to classes in dance, tennis, golf, swimming, and French.

"Miss Marta, this is becoming a habit," said Baltasar, the chauffeur. "I took you there just last week."

"That's why I want to go, because I know she'll be there this time of day."

Baltasar drove to a gated house near Virreyes. The tall, ivy-covered wall made it impossible to see inside. The only thing visible was a large wooden gate blocking the driveway and a smaller pedestrian door next to it that had a narrow screen for a security guard to peep through. They waited outside.

"Baltasar, can I bum a cigarette?"

The chauffeur offered her the pack, and they both smoked. Marta was impatient. She wanted to see her. Last week she had been picked up at exactly this time.

"The Maxima isn't here," she said anxiously.

"No," answered the chauffeur without missing a beat; he was used to waiting.

After thirteen years of searching, she couldn't hide her disappointment. No, it couldn't be *thirteen*; she herself had just turned thirteen a few months back. When had she begun the search for her birth mother? At five years of age? Six? No, thought Marta, it began at the beginning. As soon as it entered the world, the child blindly sought her mother, guided by her sense of smell. Yes, the search began nearly at the beginning. Hence it had taken Marta thirteen years to find her, and she wasn't about to lose her.

The wind blew, sweeping the leaves on the sidewalk. Clouds in the blue sky hinted at nighttime showers. The street was empty. There was no sound.

A car turned the corner. It was the Maxima. Marta began nervously snapping her long fingers. *She* would come out.

The car parked in front of the house. Marta waited, her eyes fixed on the home's gate. But this time it happened in reverse: a woman dressed in a gray wool pants suit emerged from the car. She was short and curvy. The pants fit snuggly on her hips, and her straight black hair was pulled back in a ponytail. With efficient strides propelled by low heels, the woman walked through the gate on out of their sight.

How can my mother be like that? thought Marta.

When Marta was thirteen years old, their physical differences were not what most impressed her. Some years later she would ask herself why she was tall and her mother short. Why blond? How could they be so different? Were their personalities also different? But back then Marta, still more girl than woman, did not compare her body to women's; she was not even a particularly tall teenager. It was not until she turned seventeen that she went through a growth spurt. What profoundly affected Marta was how removed she felt from this woman. She asked herself the same question as always: Why did she give me away?

"Ready to leave?"

"No," said Marta. "I'm sure she'll come out again. Remember how last time she went to her office. Why don't you get out and chum up the other chauffeur and get him to spill the beans? C'mon, Baltasar, please?"

"Not here," said Baltasar. Chauffeurs had their rules; they didn't gossip with just any old chauffeur, much less on an empty street. They had to be in a group, waiting for their employers, and then, with three or four hours to kill, they would chat with one another and share information. That's how Baltasar had discovered where this lady lived. He'd told Marta because he thought it only fair that the girl knew who her real mother was. Now he regretted it. He had not taken into account that when the girl got an idea in her head, nothing else in the world mattered to her.

"That one," Marta would cry out upon seeing a lady driving a white minivan. "She looks like a good person."

"That one," her nanny would say, pointing to a toothless vagrant, and they'd both crack up.

It took Baltasar a while to figure out the game. But bit by bit he noticed that the girl pointed to women who were undeniably blond, rich, and good-looking, while those chosen by the nanny were quite the opposite.

"She's searching for her real mother," said the nanny when finally he had felt comfortable enough to ask about the game's objective. "The problem is that she always imagines it's someone even better than our lady. I make my choices hoping the little ingrate might consider that it could be someone worse, so she realizes how fortunate she is."

From the quiet of the front seat, Baltasar began filling in the story's gaps. When he finally found her, the real mother, in a city of twenty-three million people, he couldn't resist sharing his discovery. That had been a mistake.

A few minutes later the lady came out again. This time Marta caught sight of her face before the woman ducked into her waiting car.

Marta immediately made a mental note of the facial features, knowing now she'd recognize her real mother anywhere. It did not escape Marta's notice that the woman was rather ordinary.

"Follow her! No. Leave it alone. What for? Better that we go home," Marta said in a hushed voice. "Give me another smoke, will you, Baltasar? I'll buy the next pack."

They made the return trip in silence. Marta realized that the distance between her and this woman was insurmountable, or that she at least was incapable of traveling it. That lady might be her mother, but she was also a stranger. She was above all a stranger. Had she not been informed a week ago that this was her mother, Marta easily could have passed right by her without knowing it. With the woman she had known as her mom, on the other hand, she knew the smell of her hair, the sweat of her crossed hands, the sigh of her breath when they prayed together at night, the content of her drawers, and what she had inside her purse.

Marta had been very young when she first found out. Her nanny Toña had told her after Marta had poured hot soup on Toña's uniform. "Spoiled brat," the nanny had hissed. "You can tell that you're the daughter of a nobody." It was an open secret among the help: besides her nannies, two cooks and three chauffeurs had told her the news. They told her out of anger, although Ruben, the young chauffeur, had told her in a bid to gain her confidence because he'd hoped to get between her legs.

Marta never discussed this with the woman who raised her, the woman she knew as her mother. The fear of confronting the subject was such that she never got up the nerve to try. But anything seemed possible now that her father had gotten involved with Gaby. She could not find the courage to discuss it with him either. He had always been absent, and now, with his wife dead, he had abandoned Marta.

4

The Sale

Death, in the end, is only death. We start preparing to face it from the moment we are born. We try to deny it, but deep inside we know it will come. Death is too present in life for us not to be conscious of it: an obituary, crosses on roads, the news. We live regretting death. Someone close to us dies and we may spend the rest of our lives remembering that person. The absence hurts, but that very sadness signifies that at least there was *something*, something valuable—someone whom we loved. With betrayal and with lies, on the other hand, the only thing that remains is doubt. That vacuum cannot be filled with memories; rather, it is filled with conjecture. With death we lose the present and the future, but there is always the past. With betrayal the past evaporates as well, leaving only uncertainty. With death life perhaps loses its color. With betrayal it loses its form, so that we are left floating in a vacuum with nothing to grasp on to.

Standing in front of the pool, Marta cried. Her mother's death had been a tragedy. But her father's betrayal, his turning into someone unrecognizable and acting in the most ignoble manner toward his wife, the woman who raised her, her mother—not to mention the family and the family name—leaving Marta forsaken, alone, and once again obliged to understand who she was; that was another thing altogether. *We are never prepared for betrayal,* she thought.

Marta had been sure of one thing and one thing only: she was a Tordella de la Vega. Even if she was not her mother's biological daughter, she was her father's—at least that's what she'd been told. After her mother had gone to a better place—how could people utter those words without cracking up?—Marta believed that her dad would take up his rightful role as head of the family. Instead, he had opted for the role of clown.

Standing there at the party, crying, Marta recalled how everyone around her had tried to hide her real mother's identity. Their attempts had failed. Nonetheless, Marta had never imagined that her father would marry another woman.

"There you are. I've been looking for you for a half hour," said Mau. "What happened?"

"Nothing. Memories," said Marta, wiping away her tears.

"Your face is streaked with black."

Marta started trying to rub it off with her hands.

"You're making it worse. C'mon, let's go."

In the guest bathroom, one of two nearest the *palapa*, Marta washed her face with the English lavender soap that her mom always kept on hand. The entire house was laid out in aromatherapy zones: lavender in the guest bathrooms, magnolia in Marta's room, tea rose in her mom's room, sandalwood in the guest room, orange blossom in the second guest room, jasmine in the third. Not only did each bathroom feature its own fragrant soap, Marti also ordered its corresponding tree or flower planted outside each room. Whenever they had guests, a fresh blossom or sprig was put in the room. In addition, each room had its own mural by the Oaxacan painter Francisco Carbadillo. Her detail-oriented mother, always the perfect hostess, replaced by the idiotic

Gaby; her house usurped by someone who couldn't tell the difference between magnolia and jasmine.

"Want to get high?" whispered Marta.

"I can't. I made a vow," said Mau.

"You and your vows."

Despite being a rebel, a real son of a bitch, and a complete hedonist who generally had no morals, Mau had a predilection for vows, and when he made them he always fulfilled them—in that he was unbending.

"What did you promise now?" asked Marta.

"No drugs—no pot, not even aspirin, no nothing. No whisky, tequila, vodka, liquor."

"Beer?"

"Sure, a couple pale ales are okay, but I'm giving up protein shakes."

"Why?"

"It got to the point where I was practically on a liquid diet. I'd get up hungover, go from the gym to the steam room, from the steam room to the office, gulp down a protein shake, and go party. One day I realized that I'd gone a long time without eating at a table."

"You should come to brunch tomorrow. Gaby thinks she's Lady Di. She assumes she has to keep the help busy just because they're there. It's going to be like the buffet at the Carlyle."

"Who else is staying at your house?"

"Just us. Gaby wanted to invite some of her nobody friends, but I told her I'd raise hell if they showed up. Although her daughter will be here tomorrow. I met her at the wedding, and she gave off good vibes, so I couldn't say no."

"The artist?"

"Yes," Marta said, her face returning to its carefully made-up state. "Anyway, tonight I'm going to put on a show. That's why I want you to come to breakfast tomorrow. I've decided I want to sell Villa del Mar, and I know Gaby is going to go nuts. The silly bitch thought that Dad came with a house, boat, and cars—the whole package. Let's see how much the miserable gold digger likes him now. Let's see if charity is among her virtues."

"C'mon, crazy. Are you going to leave your old man with no dough? What's he supposed to do?"

"Let him pull his own weight."

"He's never worked a day in his life."

Marta raised one eyebrow à la Maria Felix and put on her best *what do I care?* expression.

"You're a troublemaker. But your old man will land on his feet. Maybe the Hernándezes will give him a gig selling houses as an exclusive broker. He could live off those commissions. He knows everyone who is anyone."

"Honestly, I don't give a rat's ass. I mean, I'm not going to let him starve to death. He knows I'm there for him. He can even live with me if he wants, but I'm not subsidizing that bitch. So you'll come tomorrow?"

"I wouldn't miss it for the world. C'mon, let's go to the party. I'm craving a lesbian."

"I hate to break it to you, dearest, but there's not a single lesbian at this party. Maybe with enough motivation I could give it a whirl. Although now that I think about it, maybe Gaby's daughter, but she won't be here until tomorrow."

"No, silly," Mau said, choking on laughter. "A Lesbian is a Clamato and beer."

"Dude, I never know with you."

5

The Party

The waiter brought Mau a glass of Clamato and beer. It was spiced with Tabasco and lots of lime and helped Mau forget his craving for tequila. The party remained unchanged since he'd found Marta crying, looking out into the darkness. Gaby strutted about the *palapa* like she owned it. Dressed to kill, she was obviously enjoying her display of power.

Mau could understand his friend's thinking. It was not enough to be from one of the best families in Mexico; you also had to have money. True, the family name mattered. Some families managed to broker advantageous marriages thanks to their lineage, but anyone with money could buy a family name. The rules of social chess were fluid. If it had once had been a truism in the complex chess of marriage that "wife takes secretary," it was no longer so clear, especially when the secretary could be an Argentine model or a Russian ballerina. Mexico's riches had attracted Europeans from the time of the conquistadors, and that interest remained very much alive today. The number of available Europeans had grown considerably, but not so the available money. In the end the family name had to be backed up with money. The jingle of coin was the drumbeat to which every surname marched.

Now Marta's dad and his new wife would be expelled. Marta knew that she could return to the coast whenever she wanted. Mau surveyed the male guests; every last one would offer his house to Marta despite her awful reputation.

There was Alonso, the architect responsible for every house on the Pacific, and his handsome wife, both from good families. There was Carlos Rizales, the founding partner of one of the most important law firms. Fernando del Valle, consultant to three presidents and survivor of the political transition. Eduardo Garcia Garza, an industrialist from Monterrey; Mau wasn't sure what he did, but he thought it might involve steel. There was Francisco López Sanchez, a car distributor and assembly plant owner. Fred Vargas, who was in wine. Coqui, who was in coffee. Of course, some of the fortunes had diminished, but they'd managed to hold on to their properties. There were the Gonzálezes, the Torreses, the Riveros—everyone at the party was a somebody. The truth was that Pedro and Gaby, without Marta's dough, would soon be nobodies.

Mau ordered a beer. Desperate for tequila, he savored squelching his impulse the way an anorexic enjoys taming her appetite. He observed Marta looking ever so poised. She was a different person since her mother's death. Before, she'd be blasted by now or else holed up in her room watching television, cursing the world and not caring what they thought about her. But now she had a goal, and it wasn't just to get Gaby out of the way. She was going to destroy Gaby, punish her dad, then forgive him, and in the process become her mother's daughter, her grandmother's granddaughter. Mau could already glimpse the Tordella de la Vega brilliance about her: the ability to say just the right thing, to dress gracefully, to receive guests like a queen, and charm anyone. But on top of all that, Marta's grandmother and mother had done something with their lives. They were not mere social butterflies; they were queen bees, hardworking creators of beehives and honey. Marta's grandmother was largely responsible for vaccinating the majority of Mexican children; it was she who started the fashion for charity's grand dames to go into towns and administer vaccines. Soon all of Mexico started doing the same thing. And Marta's mom had her maternity clinics. Mau recalled the inauguration of the last clinic, when Marta's mom was already ill. She had looked supremely dignified wearing a scarf on her head. Mau was with them in the car when at the last minute Marti had pulled off her wig, saying that too many women could not afford to buy someone else's hair. She was always thinking about others. With that she'd put on the scarf and showed up looking even more elegant. *Did she know?* thought Mau. Did she know that Marta would start to straighten out? The black sheep of the family, the troublemaker at school, the junkie, the girl with the eating disorder, the rebel, the lost one. Mau was seeing her transform into something magnificent right in front of his eyes.

"Why are you looking at me like that?" said Marta, pulling him out of his thoughts.

"If your mom could see you . . ."

"What?"

"If your mom could see you now, she'd be proud."

"You know, Mau, you may think I'm crazy, but I believe she can see me. I believe she is watching me. My friends in Switzerland would make fun of me whenever I related the things that my nannies said. But even though I knew they were ridiculous stories, and even though I told them in part to amuse the other girls and in part because I missed my nannies, I did believe them. That stuff about the evil eye and how you'd become stiff if you caught a draft. That's the problem with being raised by the help. We never outgrow their superstitions."

Marta took in the party. It bothered her to see the guests carrying on like merrymakers. What were they celebrating? How dare they show their faces. They'd been her mother's friends. They had worshipped her, and yet here they were paying tribute to Gaby. She'd expected a certain amount of loyalty, some show of backbone, or what people call consistency. Or was it good sense? What was the word? Something like "constitution," when people didn't behave like spineless mollusks. Was it "coherence"?

She wanted her mother's friends to be sad. She wanted them to dress in black and flagellate themselves like the men who played the role of the Christ of Iztapalapa. She wanted them to take her side against her father and against Gaby the usurper. But, of course, these were the same people who attended parties for thieving ex-politicians turned businessmen.

There was Juan Martínez, who had been jailed for taking dollars from Arizmendi's kidnapper in his brokerage houses. The Sánchez Esquerras had sold the very house where over one million dollars in cash had been found. They couldn't say that they didn't know anything about the deal, because they'd had the nerve to brag about receiving the sum for the sale in cash.

Like all ecosystems, the city bred the sort of individual who could survive and reproduce in that sort of environment. Just like the desert-bred scorpions and tumbleweed, Mexico City produced people who were able to battle, live, flourish, and prosper in a place that was over-populated, poor, contaminated, and corrupt. It took a very specific individual to survive and reach the pyramid's apex: cold, highly adaptable, able to get on well with people, capable of seducing anyone. Chameleonlike beings, they were agile, mutant, and above all else they knew how to keep up appearances.

What were they doing here? Did they come for the food, the drink, or because they liked the house? They came to see and be seen, to say they'd been there, to broker deals. Marta wanted nothing to do with them. She wanted to knock them out with a move she'd learned in kickboxing class.

On the other hand, these were the same people who had watched her grow up. They were the only people she knew. Many of them had attended her parents' wedding. Marta had watched the video a little while ago. One sad afternoon she'd gone through sixteen hours of home movies without stopping; it was the only heritage she had left. The images on the screen, converted into a time machine, showed the wedding, Marta's baptism, her first steps, and featured many of the same people whom she now despised, some of whom were carrying on as if nothing had changed.

"Bring me a tequila, 'cause it's showtime. No, better yet, let's get some dice and make a game of it. Let chance decide how I'll proceed," she told Mau.

They sat down on leather seats illuminated by the light from the pool while Marta laid out the rules of the game. "If I roll high, I'll do it tiger-style. Blast the music and dance on a table. When Gaby comes to grumble, I'll throw her out while screaming at the top of my lungs that I'm selling the house."

"That spectacle will cost you two hundred thousand dollars on the sale of the house," Mau said.

"You think? Because of the scandal? You know what? It would be like a parting blow to the old Marta; it'd be the last big hurrah. Man, I haven't even changed into the new Marta yet, and I already miss the old one."

"Second option?"

"Okay, if I roll low, I'll do it serpent-style. I'll tell Alonso's wife first so that she can gossip about it, and Alonso, who's like a lousy little girl, will tell everyone. Then we can have fun figuring out if Gaby always has that sour-lemon face or if she's put it on because she's heard the news."

"I prefer that option."

"So, go on. Blow on the dice."

"What about the third option?"

"You've thought of another way?"

"Yeah, the decent option, the normal one."

Marta looked doubtful.

"The one where you inform Gaby and your dad about your plans."

"Fuck off. Do you think I'm capable of that?"

"Not really, but I wanted to see your face when I proposed it. Besides, you know I'm right. It's the decent thing to do."

"Okay, so if I roll a straight flush, then I'll do that because it would mean that the gods truly want me to reform. C'mon, blow."

Marta shook the cup and rolled five dice onto the table. It was a low roll. She would break the news serpent-style.

6

The Trust Fund

Marti had no time to spare. The cancer was spreading, and she needed to leave her affairs in order. But how was she to repair the damage done by years of negligence in just a few months? The way one repairs a broken fence, with care and money. She worked it out. Marti knew that Marta would not be able to manage all the assets. Marta had not excelled in high school or college. In fact, her daughter showed no interest in money at all, except when she went shopping. If she left things as they were, between Manuel, the administrator, and Pedro they would take everything from her daughter. Marti had to protect Marta. Manuel had overseen the business while Marti's father had been in charge, and Marti had put up with him during the time when her husband supposedly managed things. She knew that Manuel stole from them, but he was a capable manager—something that Pedro would never be—and she'd been able to control how much he took. In fact, she'd considered it part of his salary. But now it was time to get rid of Manuel. She needed to act with professionalism, offering him a good severance package so that he'd leave happily. In the long run it was the cheapest way to let him go.

She went to see Juan Órnelas Montesinos, who had been her father's attorney. His son, who had the same name, now managed the practice and helped Marti with her affairs.

"So you don't think Marta is capable?" he asked.

"Not right now, no."

"What about in ten years?"

"Oh, Juan, for God's sake, don't torture me. Who knows what'll become of her in ten years? I won't be there to take care of her." Her eyes filled with tears as she let out a cheerful laugh. "You see what I'm like. I have no imagination."

They discussed various strategies. They called in an estate specialist and agreed to establish a trust fund in perpetuity. All of Marti's estate, the company, the bank accounts, the real estate, and other assets, all of it would be put into a trust fund to be jointly managed by Juan, Father Patrick, two accountants, and Marta. Marti felt reassured knowing that if Marta wanted to do something sensible, Juan and Father Patrick would support her. In the meantime she would receive a stipend each month, as would her children if she ever had any, and the children of their children, and so on, in perpetuity.

"Should there come a time when an adviser is missing, the remaining ones will name another adviser and continue doing so successively," said the lawyer. "We have managed this type of inheritance for many years with great success. Do you remember Dionisio Gómez Sánchez? Well, he is one of the beneficiaries of Don Gustavo, who put everything in a trust fund just like the one I've laid out for you."

How was it possible that Marti's life, or what remained of it, had been reduced to this? Her maternity clinics would continue to operate. That had been the great work of her life—to give indigent people a modicum of dignity. But now her work was to ensure that little Marta would inherit her fortune. Would that girl realize what Marti had done for her? Had it been worth the effort to save her?

Marta spent the final days of her mother's life at her side, attending interminable meetings with lawyers, notary publics, accountants, and business managers.

Marta noticed that Marti's face warmed into a soft smile each time she reiterated that she was not leaving any assets to Pedro. But it was not until Marta found out about Gaby that she understood her mother's reasoning. Her mom had always known about Pedro's betrayal, and she had prepared her revenge with great care. Now it was up to Marta to carry it out.

7

The New Wife

In her first self-esteem class, they told Gaby that she needed to value herself. They spoke of the two contrary but coexisting forces yin and yang. Later she took a course on crystals and another on philosophy. She memorized her chakras and the seven types of energy. She learned to find her solar plexus and her third eye. Most of all, she learned how to breathe, because *prana* was everything.

She'd worked hard to get to where she was now. She was raised to be quiet, bathe every day, make *salsa verde*, and mop the floors. She took her first English lesson when her parents—a factory worker and a seamstress—realized that their dreams had come true. Their daughter, who had the greenish eyes of her grandfather, would marry an engineer and never need to work another day in her life.

Her parents had simple dreams: cover the rent, go to Mass on Sunday, and pay for their own funerals. For three generations, as far back as they could recall, they had lived in Morelos. Before that there was talk of a hacienda where their great-grandfather or great-great-grandmother had freed the horses and given them all to Pascual Ortiz

Rubio, a hero of the Revolution. From there they'd gone to the *ejido*, a communal farm, and then to the city. They had never lacked for anything, but they had always needed to work. Gaby's family held two words sacred: Sunday and retirement. Gaby suspected that they believed in God solely because he'd created Sunday, and anyone who could give them a day of rest had to be divine.

"When I retire," her father would say on Sunday mornings as he opened the refrigerator to count the two cases of beer that he bought without fail as soon as his Saturday shift was done, "everything will be pure pleasure."

Gaby tried to recall other words her father spoke with some frequency, but nothing came to mind. Sundays, after having breakfasted on beef head tacos, they went to Mass. When they returned from church, her father sat alone in silence, drinking one beer after another. Around six in the afternoon her mother served *pozole*, which they ate without making a sound, listening to the radio tuned to the *ranchera* station.

"It's so that we may have good dreams," her mother would say, "and energy for the week ahead." Three or four beers later, her father would lower his head onto the table. Between the two of them they would carry him to bed, leaving him in his underwear. Her father's strong and hairless body remained as motionless as a rag doll filled with lead.

Gaby rarely saw her father during the week. She'd hear him wake up early in order to punch his timecard by 7:00 a.m. She knew that the factory was far away, that her father played on a soccer team, and that he was a union member—his promotion to assistant secretary had been cause for celebration. But she knew nothing else about him. There were vacations at the company's sports complex, which had small single-family cabins, a soccer pitch, a pool, and zip line. There were uncles and a few compadres, who despite their constant presence had left no mark.

It was in a spiritual center near San Miguel de Allende that a Tibetan nun with an Argentine accent made Gaby recall her mother. The retreat lasted a week. The first night, in order to purge themselves they were given a dinner of nopal cactus juice with spirulina. Some participants managed to fall asleep on the wood cots, but the majority spent the night by the latrine, fending off mosquitoes under a star-crammed sky.

The activities began at four in the morning, which was when the stars aligned and conditions were most conducive for the flow of energy. It was difficult to be skeptical amid so many stars. From six to eight they worked: sweeping, planting, weeding, cleaning, washing, preparing a breakfast that consisted of carrot juice. Throughout the day they were only allowed to drink tea. The goal was to cleanse the body and free up the positive energy that all people had inside them but which was trapped by the awful toxins around them. They had to keep silent. The nun led them in chants, prayers, and readings during meals, frequently conducted in Sanskrit.

On the third day they each had a private interview with the spiritual leader, for which they were instructed to arrive fully purified. Three days without sleep or food guaranteed total cleansing. There were rumors that some people had snuck out into town at night for snacks. Gaby could not understand how they could be so foolish, given how much they were paying. As soon as Gaby sat with the guru, she started to cry. She tried to contain her sobbing. She had not gotten this far to waste her allotted half hour crying. Zati Satya Narayama remained completely still in front of her, seated in the lotus position with her back perfectly straight and her blue eyes nearly transparent.

"Lie down," she said in a firm voice. "Think about your mother. Recall her, and when you're finished remembering her, let her go. Your destiny is different. So is your karma. You do not have to purge yourself of her sadness. Open yourself up and accept it."

In that moment Gaby saw her mother sitting at the sewing machine, busy at the stove, asleep on the living room sofa, where she would stay "so as not to bother your dad." Late into the night, with piles of pants and blouses to mend, she'd say, "The good thing is that I never lack for work." At a rate of ten pesos, which she never increased, there were always hems to mend.

Her mom didn't know the true meaning of the words "retirement" and "Sunday," and she never asked Gaby for help because at some point she, too, realized that Gaby had a different fate.

8

The Artist

Adriana walked hurriedly toward the taxi stand at Parque México. She hated taxi-stand cabs and had left her apartment hoping to find an eco-taxi. One of those *vochitos* that she liked so much, like the Volkswagen Beetles Damián Ortega had deconstructed. Now, that was art. That was brilliant. What was more Mexican than a *vochito*? More visible? Better known? More kitschy? Damián had taken the cliché and, piece by piece, raised it high, as though the parts were floating in space— the *vocho* made universe—simply by removing the screws and gravity. Fantastic. And now there wasn't a single one on the street, so she'd have to pay three times as much for some lousy taxi to take her to the airport.

She liked the brisk early-morning air. Although she wasn't the only person on the street, there was still a calm that would soon be replaced by a filthy ruckus. She made a mental note: she should set out walking earlier, exactly at this hour, before the city awoke and while it still resembled that mythical and transparent Mexico that Diego and Frida lived in back when the volcanoes still could be seen. As she neared the orange taxis lined up along the edge of the park, a man broke from the circle where the drivers were chatting, put out his cigarette, and opened the car door.

"Toluca Airport, please."

"That'll be four hundred pesos, miss."

"Four hundred! It's only one hundred and fifty to the other airport."

"If you prefer, I can drop you off at the minibus."

"Which minibus?"

"One leaves Santa Fe for the airport every fifteen minutes."

"How much does that cost?"

"I don't know, miss, but I'll only charge you two hundred to go to Santa Fe."

Adriana scanned Mexico Avenue one last time, hoping to find a green taxi that would take her to the end of the world for a hundred pesos. She tried to recall the name of the artist who had done exactly that—traveled all the way to Tijuana in an ecotaxi, photographing and videotaping the entire trip.

"Fine, take me."

That's what she got for always booking the cheapest flight, even though her mother had offered to buy the ticket.

Adriana made sure that the taxi was taking a familiar route. Once she was certain of their trajectory, she stopped worrying. The taxi went through the Lomas area via Reforma Avenue on its way to Santa Fe. Traffic was starting to pick up. Seeing the homes of the wealthy made her think of her mother.

Adriana had drawn her mother for the first time when she was five years old. She'd already stopped painting with colors and had become interested in pencil. She had a notebook of white card stock that her mother bought for her on the first Sunday of each month. Years back her mother had realized that she needed to ration the paper because while Adriana's little hobby was not exactly expensive, it could turn into a luxury if she let the girl pursue it without limits. On the other hand, she bought her big rolls of rollout paper that she found for three pesos at La Merced. Even then Adriana made it a habit to sketch on rollout paper and then transfer her finished drawings to card stock. The first portrait of her mother showed her standing barefoot. The five toes on each foot looked superimposed, as though seen from above, because she had not yet mastered perspective. Her mother's dress was meticulously outlined and filled in with pale-blue pencil—the only color in the entire drawing. There was also an apron with a well-executed pleated waist. Adriana tried to give the face dimension by drawing a somewhat exaggerated oval. She was already painting almond-shaped eyes, pupils with irises, eyebrows, and eyelashes. She recalled how important it had been for her back then not to leave out a single element. The drawing featured ears, earrings, and her mother's hair the way she wore it: pulled back in a ponytail and fastened with two clips.

Adriana had always been a close observer of her mother, especially when she did the *quehaceres*. *Quehaceres*. What a wonderful word, she thought: those + tasks. That's what they were—tasks that had to be done every day: cleaning the bathroom, making the beds, sweeping, replacing a light bulb, paying the gas, and dusting. Tedious and seemingly trivial things that didn't merit naming.

Adriana wasn't sure if she still drew for pleasure. Perhaps, but at the same time she recognized that it was a custom she'd picked up as a girl, when she sensed that she shouldn't be a bother, that her mother already had enough work to do, and that it was better if she remained still and quiet. Drawing didn't bother anyone. Until she started drawing things that pissed off people, and she became aware of her power. But that was later.

Her mother started working when Adriana was ten years old. She took off her apron, loosened her hair, added blond highlights, and painted her eyes; eventually, she even tattooed her eyelids and the outline of her lips. Adriana had just discovered pastels. She did another portrait of her mother, softening her face, this time in three dimensions. It was a three-quarter profile, her mother's wavy and yellow hair reflecting the recent highlights, her lips painted in pink tones. She drew green and yellow sparkles in the eyes, for she'd discovered that her mom's eyes had rays, like the sun.

Adriana had learned to wash and iron her uniform and to prepare her meals. After school, at home alone, she would turn on the television, do her homework, and draw sketches of soap-opera actors. She sold one of Rogelio Guerra at school.

Around that time her mom became talkative, but it was too late. Adriana was not interested in the details of her job or in giving opinions about which dress best suited the occasion. She'd discovered books, and she had a group of friends with whom she could discuss the things that interested her: art, life, politics. She'd read Carlos Castaneda as easily as Nietzsche, and José Agustín alongside Thomas Hardy. She'd cut classes and spend entire days in the Gandhi Bookstore, drawing the old men who played dominoes. Her friends played guitar, smoked pot, and went to Coyoacán. Adriana did not talk about any of this with her mother.

Now she regretted it. Her mother was going off to live in one of these houses, and Adriana didn't know who her mother had become. She thought about getting to know her. She didn't have time. It made her sad to think that she didn't have enough time to get to know her mom, but at least she'd agreed to spend the weekend with her.

"This is where I'll leave you, miss," the taxi driver said as he pulled up to a terminal with parking spots instead of runways. "Look, that's the minibus you should take."

Counting her money carefully, Adriana thanked the driver and paid him. She had two hundred pesos left and hoped to arrive at the Tordella de la Vega home without having to hit an ATM. She thought about doing an installation with ATMs. Maybe viewing them from within. They saw us. They had security cameras. They knew our names, and they gave us money. What was the relationship between ATMs and us? Maybe she would set up an ATM that ate people's cards and then film their reactions. No, that was too *Candid Camera*. She needed something more profound. Maybe imagine an ATM loaded with dough, flirting with another one, asking it for its balance to determine if the other ATM was a good catch. Maybe a performance piece with a chain saw splitting an ATM in half, bills flying everywhere and the noise. Sparks.

9
The Surgery

From the twenty-eighth floor of Lomas Altas Hospital, located at the end of Avenida Reforma, Gaby could observe the entire city. The two volcanoes, Popo and Itza, were visible in the distance, and Gaby tried to identify at least one building. The Peli Towers in Polanco? The Reforma Tower? She could pick out the National Auditorium and Campo Marte, but the rest were indistinguishable gray and brown cubes. A thin layer of smog spread out over the entire landscape, but it was still an exceptionally clear day.

Gaby was wearing a white linen suit over a white silk blouse with wide fuchsia stripes. A thousand times over she'd heard that simplicity was synonymous with elegance. Pedro for one never stopped repeating it, which was why she'd chosen the white suit over the one with the flowery print, even though the latter seemed more cheerful and practical. This suit had to be dry-cleaned after each use. But she wanted to look elegant and full of life. That's why she'd come here. It was her secret. No one knew her whereabouts, and with a little luck they would not find out.

"A few days recovering at home," was the only thing the doctor had said.

Gaby thought of her oft-repeated mantra: *I won't get in the way.*

She could not recall exactly when she'd decided to take charge of her life. It seemed like a gradual process, a series of small steps in a clear direction; this procedure was but another small step.

Using a computer, the doctor had demonstrated how her breasts would look after the operation: large, round, sensual, defying gravity and age. He'd also give her a few injections to reduce the wrinkles on her forehead, and, he said, a little collagen on the lips and cheeks would make her appear twenty years younger.

Who could have imagined that she'd get this far? The wife of Pedro de León! Her days of worrying were finally over, and after years of scrimping she could spend her savings on frivolous things.

Until recently their encounters had been restricted to restaurants, her apartment, and that trip they'd taken to Villa del Mar. But now she would occupy her rightful place as the wife of de León, not just his lover. She would attend parties and receptions; she would travel. It was her duty to look good.

10

The Door

It seemed to Adriana that they had just taken off when they landed. The intense heat took her by surprise; it felt like being thrown inside a hair dryer. The hot-as-hell air caused her to sweat immediately, and she wanted desperately to peel off her clothes. For now, taking off her leather jacket would have to do. She rummaged through her backpack for sunglasses. The light was blinding. She had packed only a black bikini and two cotton dresses, but it took a while to find the sunglasses thrown in with everything else. Once inside the airport, which was dark and icily air-conditioned, she'd had to reverse the process, removing her sunglasses, wisely resting them on her head, and putting on her jacket. She was pleased to see a driver waiting for her at the gate.

"Señorita Ortega?"

"Señora."

From the age of twenty-two she'd insisted that people address her as señora rather than señorita, even though she was not married. This had started at her first show, when she realized that the honorific bothered her. She had not been a señorita in the virginal sense of the term for many years. Moreover, she wasn't getting married anytime soon; in fact, she didn't plan to marry ever. So if she was going to make the jump to señora—rather than mimic the unmarried teachers at her school who fancied themselves señoritas at fifty—it seemed as good a time as any. So from then on she made it a point to correct everyone. Adriana thought she caught the driver scrutinizing her hand for a ring, but she let it go. Most people were much less observant than she assumed.

Riding in a minivan that could seat twelve people and was upholstered in terry cloth, Adriana watched the bright landscape through her dark glasses. There were rows of coconut palm trees and, growing in their shade, a type of tree with thick leaves.

"What are those just under the palm trees?" she asked.

"Those are mangoes."

"Ah," she sighed, "and when are they in season?"

"The season's just ending," said the driver in his coastal accent.

"And the coconuts?"

"We have them all year round."

She remained quiet the rest of the way. After a while there were no more palm trees along the road, and she could make out the *colonias* in the distance, their dusty streets crammed with ramshackle houses built of cement blocks, corrugated tin sheets, and cardboard. *No running water or drainage,* thought Adriana while admiring the hot-pink azaleas, orange African tulips, and the golden trumpets of California poppies all thriving along the boulevard. She recalled her photo series that documented dressing rooms. Some of the images showed immense, seemingly unending closets. Some had automated clothes racks like the ones in a dry cleaner's. One had a fountain in the middle. They were monuments to excess. Then there were the servants' rooms. What could you say of them? Those closets held two wire hangers with uniforms. Their beds—discarded cots really—with hardly any linens. Charmless spaces with perhaps a little nail polish as the only decor, luxury, and comfort. Always a crucifix, a sacrificial Christ nailed on the wall to remind the servants of their lot in life. Some had a small shrine to the Virgin of Guadalupe, the miserable myth of the mother of all Mexicans—the one who abandons them while they waste their lives searching for her.

The minivan stopped at a large iron gate guarded by men wearing African safari uniforms—white pants, khaki jackets, hats with leather trim—that looked like they might have been designed by Ralph Lauren. They went along a paved driveway through lush vegetation. The palm leaves shone like traffic lights against the pure-blue sky. They came to a sort of hill, where the jungle opened suddenly onto a gigantic Hindu door, the goddess Tara with her twenty thousand arms framed by images of Shiva and Vishnu.

How had this door gotten here? It must have weighed tons. Adriana imagined the door's journey, the work of those who had crafted and designed it. No doubt it had belonged to a temple. She imagined the chain of complicity: an astute merchant who'd purchased it, or stolen it, assuring the monks they didn't really need a door but that they did need rice, and paying them enough for two years' worth of meals. She imagined the foreigners who arrived in India at the start of the last century, searching for loot to take with them, stripping the country of its treasures, creating a market for invaluable objects. It would take an army to move that door. Besides the human labor, they'd need a crane to lift it into a shipping container and a crew to make sure the precious cargo made it from India to Mexico. In the blink of a second, Adriana visualized a globe with navigation routes and millions of containers traveling between continents: food, oil, people in constant motion, and among them a sacred door in a transpacific vessel destined for Acapulco. It would be interesting to trace the journey of these supervaluable objects that were insured for incredible sums, the Picassos and Cézannes that went around the world, the luxury cars en route to Abu Dhabi. Why do we take extraordinary care of such objects? Why do we desire them so, and why do we allow thousands of human beings to perish in cross-border traffic? Man creates art, so why do we value art and not man?

Santiago Sierra did a performance piece in which he paid some Cubans to stand against a wall and "detain" it. He paid another group to tattoo a horizontal line on their backs. To drive home his point, he paid a man to live for several days at PS1 in New York. He built a wall with only a pass-through for a lunch tray. Someone agreed to do that, to live shut in behind a wall for cash.

Images of *pateras* and containers paraded in her mind. A very straight row of containers and another identical row of those open boats favored by immigrants converged at some point and began to intersperse, alternating one after the other until they formed a spiral, as though they were inside a blender that had been switched on, everything—the people and objects—broken and scrambled by the great cosmic blender.

She walked onto the *palapa* situated so high up that it looked out upon the whole sea and sky, seemingly the entire horizon. It framed the most impressive view of intense Yves Klein blues that Adriana had ever seen. An old servant dressed in white pointed her to a bedroom.

"And my mother?"

"Brunch is served at twelve, señora. You have enough time to freshen up."

"Where is the swimming pool?"

"There's one on your left and another on your right as you go down the stairs."

The room smelled of jasmine and had soft music piped in from hidden speakers. A white bedspread of Portuguese cotton covered the bed. To one side of the room, on a table crafted of dense black wood—the most beautiful table that Adriana had ever seen—a jasmine branch sat in a white vase of Japanese porcelain. She did not resist the urge to take a photo of the solitary and beautiful branch. *Someday,* she thought, *I'd like to own a table like that.* At the end of the room, a Francisco Carbadillo mural portrayed a sort of genealogical tree of evolution. There was a corn seed at the base of the trunk, then the roots, like an invitation to an underworld, the first animals, and an axolotl. Along the branches were indigenous animals—opossums, badgers and ocelots, toads and deer—implausibly paired up amid the tropical foliage and desert flora. It was an impressive work—Mexican, pre-Hispanic, and modern. It pleased Adriana not to be let down by an artist whom she considered one of the great maestros of Mexican painting.

She searched for her iPod before undressing. She'd created a floral playlist: *"Dos gardenias para ti," "En el tronco de un árbol una niña,"* and "Painting Flowers on the Wall." Then there was Tania Libertad singing *"Life's avalanche has swept you along"* in *"Flor de azalea."* Listening on the shuffle and repeat settings, Adriana put on her black bikini and went to the first pool she could find.

I can see how someone would grow accustomed to this, she thought, wanting to forgive her mom.

She removed her earbuds and dove headfirst into the pool. With the well-pitched voice of someone who has long practiced her scales, she belted out, *"Tú me acostumbraste-eee . . ."*

"Did you know that song is gay?"

Adriana turned around. A man with a sculpted body, thick beard, and bright eyes was smiling at her.

"Hi, I'm Mau," he said, extending his hand. "I assume you're Adriana."

"Yes. Hi."

"If you listen closely to the song, you'll see it's a gay lament. He tells his lover, I've grown accustomed to all those marvelous things you showed me. The key is when he says, 'I could not imagine how to love in that strange world. But I learned for you.' Then comes the loveliest part when he asks, 'Why didn't you teach me how to live without you?'"

"I always thought of it as simply a love song."

"Yes, a gay love song."

"Is there a difference?"

"For an artist you're not terribly sensitive. Imagine: the dude is seduced, turned into a cocksucker, and then abandoned. Not only does he end up crushed but a fag to boot."

"So what? At least he knows where to look for love again, right?"

Mau thought about it.

"Are you staying here too?"

"No, I'm in the Rivero house. I'm just here for brunch. Shall we?"

11

The Brunch

"Wow," said Adriana.

"Wow!" said Mau.

A magnificent buffet covered a table that was easily ten yards long. A sculpture of tropical fruits dominated the right side of the table, where platters of every fruit imaginable were laid out: papayas, watermelons, passion fruits, mangos, mameys, guavas, and pineapples, along with imported delicacies, such as kiwis, raspberries, blackberries, and blueberries. There was an assortment of cream, yogurt, honey, and three kinds of granola. In the center of the table were trays of *chilaquiles* with tomatoes and salsa, *sopes* topped with beans and salsa, enchiladas, green and red salsas, *queso fresco*, and *panela*. There was salmon and eggs Benedict, pancakes and waffles, and even sushi.

The dining table was square and could seat sixteen people, with four on each side. But only five places were set—two at each side of the table and one facing the sea. The centerpiece was a montage of seashells, some real and others ceramic or silver.

Mau and Adriana sat side by side and remained quiet, like expectant accomplices.

A waiter dressed in a white Nehru jacket offered them a variety of juices. Mau requested coffee and Adriana mandarin juice.

Gaby tried to focus on her breath while surveying the buffet. Inhale: one, two, three. Exhale: one, two, three. Hold: one, two, three, four. Inhale: one, two, three. By the time Marta had informed her that she'd rescinded the invitations to her friends, it was too late. Gaby had already ordered food for sixteen guests. She'd freeze what she could; a lot would go to waste. At least she'd arranged for a decadent spread. Comme il faut. She'd taken pains to learn how, and now she gazed upon her creation with pride. It had all the recommended elements from the books she'd read. Scale: two tall decorations surrounded by low ones framed the centerpiece. Colors: coordinated to match the Pacific palette. Variety: something for every taste—vegetarian, dietetic, sweet tooth, spicy, and for sensitive stomachs. There was not a single fly; it had been her flash of genius to spray the table with insecticide.

Adriana watched Gaby with disbelief. Was that her mom standing in front of the table, the royal palms that formed a wall of straight, white-painted trunks behind her?

"How are you, *mijita*?" Gaby said, embracing Adriana and kissing her on the cheek. She'd told herself a thousand times not to address Adriana as *mijita*. She knew it didn't sound right, but it was a hard habit to break, and now it was too late to take it back. "The trip was okay?"

"Yes, Ma, thanks," said Adriana. "Well, I did have to take a taxi to Santa Fe, which cost almost as much as the plane ticket. I hadn't been to Santa Fe in a while. How it's grown! It's a changed city!"

"It's cool, right? My parents moved there a few years back, and they never left," Mau said to Adriana, before turning to the host. "Gaby, this is some meal you've put together. Marta said it would be good, but you've outdone yourself."

"Thanks, Mau. You're always such a gentleman."

Adriana didn't recognize her mom's voice. It had the same shrill tone as always, but there was something new about it, very fake and rehearsed.

It hurt Adriana to see her mom like this, with her hair dyed blond and her skin tanned. She wore a brown bikini under a matching tunic with Indian-style embroidery that was practically see-through, and sandals with gold heels.

"Mommy, what's going on? There's something different about you," said Adriana, unable to contain herself. *She's had work done,* Adriana thought, immediately conjuring up the image of the artist Orlan and her horns. For a moment she perceived her mother with a demon's face.

Gaby felt her daughter's penetrating stare. "It must be my hair, sweetie. I've been going to a new salon." She lowered her sunglasses to shade her eyes, as though shielding herself against kryptonite. "Have they offered you juice? It's the healthiest and the least fattening. Oh! I forgot to ask for nopales juice. They say it's great against cancer."

Pedro came to the table wearing dark-blue cotton Bermuda shorts, a white polo shirt, and white moccasins. He looked like a ship's captain. He sat next to his wife and took her hand, which she removed under the pretext of rearranging a silver shell.

Marta made her entrance wearing a violet bikini and an open knit shawl tied around her hips. Her nails still were painted black, and she had traces of makeup. She greeted each one of them with a kiss and took her place at the table.

"We haven't all been together since the wedding," said Pedro, trying to break the ice.

When they came by to offer her juice, Marta asked for Marlboro reds. She lit a cigarette and, exhaling a good bit of smoke, said without a trace of irony, "Oh yes, such a beautiful ceremony. Do you remember?" Looking at Adriana, she inquired in a friendly tone, "What have you been up to since then? I saw your book on dressing rooms. I liked it. Had I known, I would have offered you my mother's. It's not as big as some of the ones in your book, but it was done in very good taste. I would have liked to have pictures of it. I know you did the work with a different purpose in mind—as a display of opulence from what I gather. But I swear to you that my mom had—I don't know—thirty or sixty tailored suits, all beige, all Chanel, Céline, or Gucci, all nearly identical, hung impeccably like a row of soldiers or nuns in a convent. Personally, if I could look at a picture of those suits the way I remember them, I'd want to keep it. I think that's the reason they let you take them: people see themselves reflected in their dressing rooms, and they like that. They're a type of portrait."

"Yes, and that's exactly the type of work I'm displaying now. The exhibit is called 'Self-Portraits.' Some are oils, others collages. The oils are two yards by a yard and a half in size and might be composed of an individual's e-mail inbox or their computer's boot-up screen, while the collages are of receipts or account statements. I painted the Facebook page of a friend and the Gmail page of the gallery owner. I made one collage with a year's worth of my mom's receipts." She expected to get a reaction from Gaby, but there was none. "Because that's what we are, right? We are who writes to us and whom we write to; we are who is in our address book, how we organize our desktop. It becomes something very intimate."

"Yes, and they have a certain transient nature as portraits go because in ten years, it won't be the same. So you're also capturing time."

"I'd like to see them," said Mau.

"I'm going to New York on Monday. The opening is on Friday, so cross your fingers. Do you want to come?"

She immediately regretted making the offer, because she realized that for these people, going to New York was like going to Polanco.

"Ah, my little one," said Gaby. "I'm just glad you're not doing things with nudes and homosexuals. Do you remember the Biennial you took me to? It was all naked men and perverts. Horrifying."

Marta started blowing smoke circles. No sooner did they form than the breeze blew them apart. "Personally, I adore homosexual art," she said, popping a smoke circle with her finger. "Any day now, with the dough I'll make from the sale of the house, I'll buy some of it. A Francisco Toledo or a Julio Galán. In any case my art dealer says that type of work holds its value. And, of course, Zárragas."

"Marta, please! Let's not talk about that now," said her father.

Marta started to puff up like a fighting cock but stopped in midair and unruffled her feathers without saying what she'd intended. "You're right, Daddy. It's bad form to discuss money at the table. Why don't we go on the boat? Mau, Adriana, are you coming?"

Mau immediately rose from the table. Adriana considered what to do while finishing up her mandarin juice. She'd never been on a yacht. The temptation was too much.

"I'll see you in the afternoon, Ma," she managed to say while following Marta and Mau.

12
The Wedding

On one of the patios of Hacienda de los Morales, the justice of the peace was reading Melchor Ocampo's *Epístola* and declaring the bride and groom man and wife. Sylvia and another of Gaby's friends attended the ceremony, along with two of Pedro's friends and his sisters, as well as their husbands. Adriana and Marta stood behind the chairs so as not to stick out.

"Hi," said Marta. "We haven't been introduced. I assume you're Gaby's daughter."

"Yes, Adriana. Hi."

Adriana put out her hand, and they eyed each other in silence. Both were dressed in black. Marta was thrown off because she'd expected a kiss on the cheek. Marta wore a Chanel suit with a skirt that had obviously been shortened, and a black hat with a veil. Adriana sported black pants and a mannish, untucked black cotton shirt.

There was a table for twelve people in the middle of the patio. Adriana was flanked by Sylvia, whom she detested, and her mother's other friend, who also worked in real estate. After five minutes she had nothing left to say to them.

Marta sat between her two aunts. She lit a cigarette and downed a tequila in one shot. She ordered another and, while she waited, put out her cigarette and headed toward the bathroom. Adriana observed all this and followed behind her.

"What's your sign?" asked Marta when Adriana entered. She was rolling a joint.

"Capricorn. You?"

"Leo."

"Did you know that when the Egyptians named the constellations, the sky was different from when we were born?" Adriana said. "Technically, it has been shifting, and we were born under a prior constellation."

"Really?" asked Marta surprised. "No, I didn't know that. I thought the Greeks named them."

"I'm not sure; I don't know anything about the zodiac. That's what I was told by a sculptor who used constellations in his work and knew a lot about astronomy. In any case the Egyptians and Greeks were contemporaries, right?"

"But regardless of the sky under which you were born, if from the time you're a kid they tell you that you're an Aquarius and that you're this and that, in the end you end up believing it and behaving that way."

"Probably," said Adriana. "I've never given it serious thought."

Marta finished rolling the joint.

"Look," said Adriana, "there are six billion people on earth. If you divide that by twelve months, that's five hundred million people with similar personality traits and similar things happening to them every week, according to the zodiac. Can you imagine? Twenty-five times the population of Mexico City is Cancer or Leo."

All her life people had told Marta that she embodied the Leo personality. Leos need attention. Leos are loud. Leos roar. Leos let their claws out when they're angry. Unable to fully imagine it, she pictured five hundred million Leos, all born like her in August and conceived more or less in December. Marta, who had always been made to feel special, now found herself in the company of millions and millions of similar beings and, on top of that, under the wrong sky. What sign was she, then?

Minutes before, Gaby had proposed a toast. She talked about forming a family and how she hoped her daughters would get along like sisters. *Fucking whore. She doesn't know what's in store for her,* Marta had thought.

"I never looked at it like that," Marta said, lighting the joint and taking a few hits before passing it to Adriana.

They remained silent. Marta remembered how a shaman in Zipolite once told her that her totem was an osprey and that it was a very powerful sign. Her friends had made fun of her because, traditionally speaking, your totem is the first animal that passes close to you after birth, and since all of them had been born in Mexico City, the only totems possible were a crow, a rat, or a dog. Marta didn't say anything. She didn't tell them that she was born in Coronado, where ospreys were common.

Marta told Adriana that her totem was an osprey. They both laughed the desperate, awkward laugh of the stoned.

13

Table Talk

Gaby was furious. Ignoring the sea view, she turned to the untouched buffet and said, "Your spoiled daughter didn't eat a thing."

"Neither did yours," said Pedro.

Gaby grabbed her plate and headed for the food. She served herself red and green *chilaquiles*, an enchilada, two slices of smoked salmon, and half of a toasted bagel. To top it all off, she added an egg Benedict and two strips of bacon. She returned to the table, adjusted one of the shells, and began eating.

Gaby had spent years thinking positively and imagining good outcomes. How many times had she imagined herself here? Living in this house that she'd come to know barely a year ago, thinking about marrying Pedro, wondering if she could conquer him, as though he were the summit of a mountain. How many more steps were needed to reach the top of Everest? Yet here she was. She had reached unimaginable heights. Still, digging into her dish, she couldn't help but admit to herself that she was unhappy.

So that's why he liked me, she thought. *He knew I came cheap.*

She stuffed another mouthful of *chilaquiles* into her mouth. She knew it disgusted Pedro to watch her eat. It bothered him to see her switch the fork between her hands or leave the flatware on the side after she finished, as though attempting to show manners she clearly didn't possess. He never let her forget that.

He'd put up with it once, and Gaby had looked up to him, eager to learn his ways. She knew that Pedro loved her only because he felt worshipped. After all, didn't she blow him with absolute dedication whenever he wanted? As though it was the only thing in the world she desired. Marti had never blown him. Pedro told her that Marti would not even touch his dick. Naturally, having it all, Marti had not needed to worry about satisfying him. He, on the other hand, had gone through life trying to please his wife, with no success.

Was this what marrying Pedro had made her? To think she'd been the one who'd insisted—who'd demanded—the marriage! Nothing had turned out the way she'd hoped.

Her plate was empty.

"Waiter," Gaby yelled sharply, snapping her fingers. "Waiter!"

"Don't snap your fingers," said Pedro, who had been watching her the entire time.

"I'll do what I want in this house, which truth be told is neither mine nor yours. Besides, this is the last day these servants will see me."

"But not I," said Pedro.

"No, not you."

14

The Boat

Marta, Mau, and Adriana drank Lesbians and tequila on the deck of the yacht.

"I love these cups. They're like the ones for toddlers," said Mau.

"Yeah, my mom was great with this sort of stuff. She would have gone ballistic if anyone stained her boat, but she also didn't want to be the typical party pooper, so she bought these cups with lids designed for kids. They used them to serve anything that might leave a stain."

"It's pristine. You got it recently?" Adriana said, admiring the wood finishes, the meticulously designed doors, the whiteness of the lacquer, the shine of the chrome.

"The boat?" asked Marta absently. "Some ten years."

"I thought it was new!" Adriana said.

"God, no. They stopped making this model three years ago. Look, now they make the windows longer, see?" Mau said, pointing to other yachts in the marina.

"Yeah, damned Italians. They're always updating details so we feel screwed," said Marta.

"You feel screwed?" said Adriana. She was completely captivated by Marta. It wasn't the first time she'd seen her, but it was the first time she'd observed her up close in bright daylight and nearly nude. She was long and bony like a Giacometti. There was a certain harmony about her that stood out. A gracefulness. She seemed filled with light.

"Yes and no. In some ways, yes. But in other ways, no. I don't know. You?"

"Me? Totally screwed. There's nothing to be done about it, so I've grown used to it."

"Well, you've got a great attitude for someone who's screwed," said Mau. "How did you learn to sing so well?"

Adriana was relieved that he'd changed the subject. She had a well-rehearsed script about her childhood that she could recite with aplomb. But she was starting to feel the tequila. She realized that she was drunk, and yet the last thing she wanted was to stop drinking. Mau and the first mate made sure that both women were topped off.

"I learned to sing in church. I was in the choir." It was one of Adriana's most pleasant childhood memories: the cool church air, the warm sound of guitars, the upbeat songs about Jesus fishing and the sun-kissed grains of golden wheat.

The first mate announced to Marta that the snacks were ready, and the captain asked her if she wanted to go closer to the shore. Marta said yes, and the boat anchored right off a small, busy beach. The incessant comings and goings of fishing boats transporting tourists caused Adriana to feel vertigo. On the beach all the restaurant stands advertised the same menu: clams, *ceviche*, *tiritas* of red snapper, lobsters, prawn quesadillas, and grilled shrimp. Brown-skinned people and fat bodies bathed near the edge of the sand. A group of kids who looked like refried beans dove headfirst from a cement jetty. Adriana could hear their laughter. One of the food shacks was called Lili Cipriani. She recalled the Venice Biennial, where a few years back she'd exhibited a photo that went completely unappreciated. There were two other yachts anchored near the shore. Mau and Adriana waved to their passengers.

Inside, luxury; outside, poverty. Inside, white; outside, a thousand shades of sand and earth. Inside, exclusivity; outside, the masses. Always surrounded by contrasts. Mexico was nothing if not loud, dissonant, and high contrast. So much color wasn't necessarily happy or bright, but it caught your eye. You never got used to such red reds, such bright yellows, such spicy salsa, and the emptiness, thought Adriana. *Perhaps I move between shades of gray, but for these people, from the impeccable white deck of the ship, a drop of color must be an incredible contrast.* She thought about how water got muddied when you dipped a paintbrush in it. In that first instant the paint doesn't want to mix. It remains intact, forming spirals, but then you shake the brush and it becomes uniform. What this country needed was someone to shake the paintbrush and finish mixing it up. For the time being, from where she was sitting there was only black or white, rich or poor. There were no grays. She started to feel uncomfortable and regretted having confided in them as though they were her friends when she barely knew them. She closed her eyes. The tequila, the sun, and the ship's movement made her nauseous.

They moved to a table at the back of the yacht, where there was shade. Adriana nibbled on some salted crackers and felt better. Then she devoured the *ceviche* with eagerness. The freshly caught fish was delicious precisely because it did not taste fishy. At least it didn't taste like the fish she loathed as a child, which her mother bought on sale and fried up with garlic. The bright combination of chopped tomato, onion, cilantro, olives, and lemon juice delighted her palate. She also tried the strips of red snapper marinated in lemon. The oily avocado helped stabilize her nausea. She drank some more frozen tequila, thick as honey.

"Aren't you mad at me?" Marta asked her out of nowhere.

"Me?" Adriana said, having no idea what Marta was talking about.

"I've decided to sell the house, and your mother will no longer be able to stay there. Maybe you hadn't realized. Gaby only found out last night."

"No, I didn't know. You don't have to sell it, do you? Couldn't you just tell her she's no longer welcome? But why would I be angry?"

"I don't know. Maybe your mom thought my dad was loaded, so now she'd be rich."

Adriana reflected on that. She thought about her mom without money, without breast implants, without the ridiculous things she'd done since meeting Pedro. But no, the transformation had begun with Sylvia.

"I don't know. Do you think she married your old man just for the dough?"

It gave Adriana a certain pleasure to think of her mother failing; in her imagination, Gaby without money would reestablish a certain order.

"No, silly. She married him for his pretty face," replied Marta.

"Well, he is handsome," said Adriana.

"You know what I mean."

"Sure, sure, I know," said Adriana, "but I'm not sure that it was just about money."

That comment bothered Marta. To her it was obvious that Gaby was nothing more than a low-class cow. She refused to entertain the idea that the marriage between her father and Gaby was a case of true love, like in some soap opera. Not wanting to make more waves, Marta raised her glass, and the three of them toasted. They went back on deck to laze in the sun. The captain raised anchor and steered the ship toward the horizon. Marta asked Mau to put some sunscreen on her. Adriana watched them. With their perfect, tanned bodies, they looked like an ad in a fashion magazine. He had Greek proportions, like a sculpture. She was long and lithe with seemingly endless limbs. Only her feet were perhaps a tad too bony. However, the boniness lent a glorious effect to her hands. While she watched, Adriana spread 60 SPF sunscreen on her dull skin. Mau finished applying sunscreen on his friend and offered to do the same for Adriana.

"No, thanks. Why don't I put some on you? I give good massages."

Mau lay down and Adriana knelt by his side. Marta watched them from the corner of her eyes. Adriana had strong arms; she obviously used them in her work. She had squat hands with short nails and square fingers. Her grayish skin had unseemly black hairs. *She should get electrolysis,* Marta thought. She couldn't imagine Adriana wearing any jewelry—maybe the occasional leather bracelet like they wore in Coyoacán. No doubt she'd worn those when she was younger. She was half hippie.

Marta would not have knelt next to Mau. She would have straddled his back and finished the massage in two minutes. But not Adriana; she kept at it in a rhythmic fashion, as though Mau were one of her artworks and she were completely engrossed in the moment, focused not on herself but on him and on the work at hand. Marta knew that she could never submit and focus like that. She would be on to the next thing, to bed if she wanted to seduce him, or tickling him if it was a friendly back rub, like in Mau's case. But Adriana had said, "Do you want me to give you a massage?" and she was doing it in earnest.

Marta felt jealous of Mau. She'd like someone to touch her that way. She'd like to feel useful hands on her back. She wanted to ask Adriana but didn't dare. *Fuck,* she thought. *I'm starting to respect her.*

Adriana finished the massage. The three of them napped until the yacht stopped in front of a cliff.

"Ready?" said Marta, stretching.

"What are you going to do?" asked Adriana. She did not trust the ocean. The others were getting ready to dive in right from the deck.

"There's the house," said Mau. "We're going to swim to it. It's time to get some exercise."

"No," Adriana responded quickly. "You go ahead. I'll return to the marina."

"Are you sure?" they asked at the same time.

"Absolutely."

15

The Siesta

Adriana arrived at the house after dusk, tired from her day in the sun.

"Have you seen my mom?" she asked a servant.

"She went out for a walk."

"Would you let her know that I'm going to lie down for a while and ask her to wake me for dinner?"

The servant nodded.

She entered her bedroom. A fresh jasmine blossom spread its aroma in the coolness of the air-conditioned room. Feeling the effects of the sun and alcohol, Adriana took off her bikini, lay naked between the clean sheets, and fell asleep.

Gaby returned from her walk full of energy. Exercise always did her good. The blood irrigated her brain and helped her think. She walked into her room's grand marble shower. It was the prettiest bathroom she'd ever been in. The first time she'd come to the house, she and Pedro had made love like uninhibited youngsters in this shower. She hadn't had the work done on her breasts yet—she looked much better now—but even then she had not been unsatisfied with her body. They had been in love. Marti was on her deathbed in Houston. Pedro had returned to Mexico for business, and Gaby began picturing herself as the future Señora de León.

In the shower Gaby noted with satisfaction her shapely thighs and perfectly round breasts standing at attention. Her belly was practically nonexistent. She shouldn't have stuffed herself at breakfast, but it had been years since she'd eaten until she was full. One day was not going to ruin her. She resolved to dine on celery with lemon juice and return to her breakfast routine of black coffee and a poached egg.

She needed to speak with Pedro and lay out the rules for the "new situation." That's how she decided to refer to getting kicked out on their asses by his spoiled-brat daughter. Pedro and she could—should—overcome the situation. What choice did they have? Her friend Sylvia had warned her, "Watch out for Marti. She may be a society lady who dotes on her maternity clinics, but she's got her hand in everything. Nothing gets past her. When I worked there, she better than anyone knew everything that was going on. Not a day went by that she didn't have a word with us."

Marta was in the south pool watching the last rays of sun. Mau had gone home to take a siesta, leaving her to think about her dad and his betrayal. She considered marriage a farce and never felt a twinge of guilt for her affairs with married men. But she did not think of herself as a home wrecker—her little sexual adventures were harmless.

What had her father done besides sleep with another woman? Didn't Marta realize that men had their needs and the right to satisfy these? What exactly was her dad's great sin? Was it taking a lover? Or was it marrying Gaby six months after her mother's death, letting the whole world know that he did not love Marti and that she was replaceable?

"I can't be alone," her father had told her, trying to justify his imminent marriage.

"I'm not asking you to be alone, Dad. I'm asking you not to marry her. Not to bring her home. Not to imagine that everything will be the same or that Gaby can replace Mom. Understand? If you marry her, you'll have to leave this house."

He'd married Gaby. Now she was alone.

16

The Mountain

Marta woke up early. She'd asked Santa Claus for a little brother, even though they had made it clear to her on several occasions that Santa did not give little brothers, that his elves in the North Pole only made toys.

Marta replied with the confused logic of a seven-year-old. "Well, didn't you say that Santa is the Baby Jesus? If he's the Baby Jesus, isn't he God? That's what you told me. And if he's God, he can do anything. That's what you always tell me."

Her mother sighed. Marti didn't want to disappoint her, but she knew that God behaved in mysterious ways when it came to bringing children into the world.

Marta had wished with all her might for a sibling, someone she could play with. She was the only one in her class who didn't have siblings. "The only *unique* one," her father had once said in a teasing tone, but also hoping to make her feel special.

Even at that age Marta realized that Christmas at her house always was and always would be a sad occasion. Her paternal grandparents had long ago ceded the holiday to their in-laws, who had more pull.

Every year they took a cruise to avoid feeling lonely, but Marti refused to go along. After Marti's parents had died, they spent Christmas by themselves.

On the twenty-fourth the three of them had dinner alone: turkey, *romeritos*, and cod. The servants ended up eating most of it. The kitchen table, around which sat more than a dozen employees, was where the real feast occurred. They, on the other hand, sat in silence and barely ate. Pedro would take progressively bigger gulps of wine, looking forward to his cognac and cigar by the fireplace.

Marta could not read her father's mind, but she knew what her mother was thinking. As soon as the nightly pilgrimages of the Virgin started, Marta watched her mom's spirits decline in inverse proportion to the increase in her activity. The pilgrimages occurred during the entire year but really picked up in mid-November, when every night for what seemed like the entire night you could hear the pilgrims' steps, the *matachín* dancers' jingle bells, the women's prayers, the loudspeakers blaring instructions, and from time to time the sirens of patrol cars directing the procession. That's when Marta's mother would shift into overdrive, organizing *posadas*, blanket-collection drives, gift exchanges, *pastorela* nativity dramatizations at her maternity clinics, and two pilgrimages to La Villa—one for the maternity clinics and the other for the office—each with its own private Mass in the chapel.

The following day, Christmas Day, they'd fly to Vail. Her mom would inevitably fall ill upon arrival and spend the time until New Year's recuperating. Marta had a great time skiing with her dad and his friends. There was nothing she enjoyed more than gliding down the slopes with him. Both were excellent skiers and amused themselves on the lifts by watching the others and comparing their outfits.

Descending the slopes with her dad, Marta felt herself to be in good company. They made a pretty pair: she with her snug pants and loose hair; he looking like an Alpine ski instructor with his tousled hair and overalls cinched at the waist.

Nothing pleased them more than to be mistaken for Americans or Europeans.

"You're Mexican? Really?" their lift companions would ask, surprised. "You don't look Mexican."

They'd flash their Colgate smiles and let themselves be admired, believing that they represented their home country well and enhanced its reputation.

They'd meet up with her father's friends for lunch at the mountainside restaurant. They tended to ski the last runs as a group. Marta loved being part of a pack of expert skiers who attacked the slopes at full speed.

Once, when her mom was already sick, a stranger mistook Marta and her dad for a couple. Marta noticed how her dad's face lit up, first with pride for being considered young enough to be with a woman of twenty, and then with shame for seeing his daughter in a sexual light. Marta was pleased to catch the desire in her father's eyes, but it lasted less than an instant. The next minute her father took off and stayed farther ahead than usual.

17

The First Marriage
(of the New Wife)

How many mistakes can one person make? Gaby could not decide if it was her destiny or her responsibility. Everything good and bad that happened in her life—was it her fault or her fate?

She had come to believe—after all those classes, all that effort—that she was mistress of her destiny and that her attitude and actions could make things go her way. Consequently, she had managed to overcome her first failed marriage. She'd become accustomed to the loneliness, the blame, the deep sense of failure, as though these were lice she could not get rid of, or an incessant itch. She'd married an engineer, becoming the first in her family to make a match with a college graduate. She finished high school. She knew she was pretty.

Small sorrows are easily concealed. From her window on Calle Pilares, she could see the unceasing traffic passing by day and night. The two buildings in front blocked the sun. Their apartment had a bedroom and a small office they would convert into a nursery when the time came. Its open design combined dining and living spaces in one room. Upstairs on the roof terrace there was a laundry area and clotheslines.

Pablo left early for work. She didn't get up. He had told her repeatedly that she didn't need to prepare him lunch. His company had a cafeteria, and when they got tired of the food there they ordered good quesadillas from a lady out front.

Gaby tried to wake up as late as possible. She had loads of spare time. Her parents' dream that she not need to work had become her nightmare. She'd do all the household chores in a half hour. At the market she'd purposely forget items so that she'd have to go back. She'd walk around the block, hoping to make friends with someone. In the afternoons she entertained herself watching soap operas. Not having a life of her own, she fervently followed the lives of their characters.

She missed her hometown of Morelia. She'd always had plenty to do there and knew everyone in the neighborhood, her school friends and her cousins. But it was so expensive to chat by phone that she rarely talked to them anymore. She limited herself to speaking with her mom every two weeks.

She believed everything would pass because they kept telling her it would—not that she complained, for she never complained. It would pass, like the cars moving down her street, like the jacarandas and the rainy seasons, over the course of time without her needing to do anything about it.

The kisses and caresses she'd shared with Pablo when they were courting after their weekly movie or dinner out turned into the nightmare of sex that started after five days at an ocean-view hotel in Acapulco. Behind pulled curtains and under white sheets, Pablo spread her legs and shoved it in with determination, as though he were preparing to score a goal. His face reminded her of a tense rabbit. When Gaby was certain that she was pregnant, that it wasn't just the smog that made her nauseous, Pablo continued taking her in the same way.

One of the things she'd most enjoyed about Pablo was that he had so many friends. He always invited one or two over for dinner during the week and six or seven on the weekends. These dinners gave meaning to her life. Gaby took pains preparing dips, one chipotle and one oyster, which they always praised, and serving the coldest beer and the best Cubas Campechana with exactly the right amount of lemon, mineral water, and Coke. She would stay in the kitchen while the men talked or played dominoes. She felt lost during the day but knew what to do as soon as Pablo and his friends arrived.

When Adriana was born, Gaby's only request was that they baptize her in Morelia. And that's what they did. Pablo invited ten friends, who did nothing but drink over two days. Gaby, on the other hand, felt distant from her friends. Between the marriage, moving to the capital, and having a child, they no longer had anything in common.

The child changed her life. Having pacifiers, bottles, and diapers on hand became her avocation. People smiled at her when she strolled down the street. They gave her oranges in the market. One day the neighbor with a two-year-old invited Gaby to her house, and from then on they watched soap operas together every day while their children played. Gaby was no longer alone.

True, she was too tired to welcome Pablo's friends with the same energy as before, but she did it anyway. True, it bothered her that they hung around, getting drunker and louder, until four in the morning when her daughter got up three times during the night, and Gaby barely slept a wink. True, she sought excuses for not having sex with her husband.

"What if I get pregnant again?"

"Take precautions."

"You take precautions!"

"How dare you! You want me to use a condom? Are you a whore? You know I don't like them. Why are you so dense? Bring me a Cuba."

This is how he concluded all arguments: "Why are you so dense? Bring me a Cuba." And she always did.

But then Pablo stopped inviting over his friends. He started getting home late. He'd leave a trail of clothes from the door to the bed. Always in the same order: first his shoes, then his suit, then his belt, which sometimes lay coiled like a viper and other times remained in his pants, and lastly his shirt. Had Gaby seen him come to bed, she would have witnessed a man in his undershirt, underwear, and socks. But she never saw him. In the morning when she got up, Pablo had already gone. She'd put out a clean suit, a pressed shirt, and everything else he needed the night before. When she got up, she would pick up his trail of clothes.

Christmas was nearing, and Gaby wanted to know if they'd be going to Morelia. Her parents had not seen little Adriana since the baptism, and even though her mother offered to visit them, Gaby felt like returning home. Sunday was the only day they spent together, if there were no soccer matches or bullfights. Pablo never missed a corrida and had been a Máquina del Cruz Azul season ticket holder for years.

They were saving up to buy a car. The day after Adriana was born, Pablo had said, "We're going to need a car so we can take her to visit your parents." Since then Gaby had been waiting for the day he brought home a car. She had done her part. She spent the bare minimum, and since Pablo's friends stopped coming over, she'd reduced their expenses by 60 percent, including what she spent on Adriana. That Sunday she raised the subject of money, hoping to guide the conversation from there to discussing their Christmas plans.

"I've been saving," she said. "Maybe we can put a deposit on the car."

"Don't bother me now."

She decided to resume the discussion on Monday because that was the day Pablo got home earliest, unless there was a game of American football, in which case he got home after midnight. When he didn't arrive, Gaby supposed there was a game on, but she decided to wait up on the sofa anyway.

"Have you thought about the car?" she asked, half-asleep.

"Don't be a nag," Pablo responded, noticeably drunk.

"You said—" she muttered in a barely audible voice.

"You said, you said," Pablo mimicked her, and then burped. "Yes, *I said*. So what? The only thing you know how to do is ask for things. Where do you think I get the money to pay my expenses, huh? You no longer spend money, right? You don't eat out, you don't drink. But what about me? You think I don't get hungry—and not just food, my dear, huh? Because man does not live on bread alone, you know? You want to wait up for me? Well, here I am right in front of you. You want to go to your parents? Go. But don't come back here, do you understand? Pablo Ortega is telling you not to come back!"

Then, as if she weren't even there, Pablo took off his shoes, pants, suit, and shirt, went into their bedroom, and slammed the door.

Gaby remained motionless on the sofa. Was that Pablo? Was that her husband? She stayed a long while without knowing what to do and finally fell asleep. When she woke, it was because Adriana needed feeding. The following day she spoke with her mom. Gaby told her they weren't coming for Christmas, and there was no reason for them to make the trip to the capital. Then she made up a story about wanting to spend the holidays at home and start their own traditions.

She spent Christmas alone with Adriana. When the child fell asleep, Gaby put the gifts she'd bought for her—a doll and some coloring pencils—under the tree. That night Pablo did not come home. Or the next night. Or the one after that. He came back after New Year's to pick up his things and leave the apartment. Gaby watched him, stunned. The only thing that occurred to her was to say, "And our daughter?"

"What do you want from me? You want me to say good-bye? Don't worry about the girl; I'll keep seeing her. She'll understand when she's old enough. Listen, and don't push it. I'm no asshole. I'll pay your rent and give you some money for expenses. But don't ask for more."

He slammed the door and left.

For another three weeks Gaby pretended that she still had a husband. Her life hadn't changed that much without him. When she finally informed her parents that Pablo had left, they came to visit.

"Come back to Morelia, *mijita*," said her mother. "You never lacked for anything in our house."

If Gaby went back to her parents, Pablo would stop paying the rent and child support. She would need to find work and help out with expenses. Her parents had aged seemingly overnight. It was as though seeing their dream vanish—learning that their daughter did not have the life they'd imagined—had stretched their skin to the point where it was now too big on them.

"It's better that I stay here," she told them. "I've made a life here; I need to move on." She didn't know the shape of this life she claimed to have made. But she was clear on one point: she could not return to her parents' house. They'd already done all they could for her. They had a right to their retirement and their Sundays.

18

The Dandy

The first time she saw him was in an art gallery.

Adriana always knew of three or four exhibits that they could attend. Frankly, the more Gaby saw of these shrill music videos, doodles, boxes, neon tires, and inner tubes, the less she understood it all. She went because she had nothing better to do. Besides, they didn't charge admission, and they served wine. It was better than watching soap operas. They didn't mingle with anyone, choosing to remain aloof among people who thought that a steam cloud made from water used to bathe corpses was something cool.

Sylvia had already spoken to Gaby about Don Pedro de León, her first boss, husband of Marti Tordella de la Vega. She said he had so many properties that it took an office of ten people just to manage them. Sylvia had started off as a receptionist, and in a few years became rent manager for three buildings in Polanco. Don Pedro managed the properties to ensure they were well maintained and always rented. Sylvia quit working there after Don Pedro refused to give her a raise, and she realized that she should be earning three times what he paid her. Gaby had seen pictures of him in the gossip magazines. The very handsome gentleman was always attending exclusive weddings, horse races, and regattas. Not art exhibits where any good-for-nothing could get in. That's why she was surprised to see him.

"Isn't that Don Pedro de León?" she whispered into Sylvia's ear. The pleats of his gray wool pants were so pressed it was as though he had just put them on, and he had on brown chamois shoes and yellow socks, which, although you wouldn't think they'd match, gave him a cheerfully elegant air.

In a series of small, discreet steps, they moved too close for him to possibly ignore them.

"Don Pedro!" exclaimed Sylvia, feigning complete surprise. "How have you been?"

"Sylvia, how are you? I see things are going well for you."

"Don Pedro, you are always so kind. How is Doña Marti? Please send her my regards," said Sylvia, turning to Gaby to introduce them.

"Gaby, I've spoken to you about Don Pedro. He was always generous with compliments to the girls in the office. If he'd been as generous with salaries, I'd still be working for him."

"A pleasure," Gaby said, extending her hand to him.

"That's business, Sylvia. You understand, business is business. Tell me, what are you doing now?"

"I'm handling one of the penthouses in the Olmos building in Santa Fe."

"We are developing the Alamos, but the Olmos is sales, right?"

"That's right, Don Pedro," replied Sylvia with pride.

"Good, Sylvia, very good. I always knew that you would go far," he said, smiling pleasantly and bowing his head a few inches. "Now, if you'll excuse me, I need to speak to someone."

"He acted like we were tying him down," said Sylvia after he'd walked away. "Did you notice how he spoke to me? Any time he sees me, he has to put me in my place."

"You did make a point of saying that he didn't pay you enough."

"He didn't pay me well! Had I stayed with him, I'd still be living with my mother and not about to close my first deal."

Two weeks later Sylvia sold the penthouse. The manicurist at her salon had gossiped to her about the wife of a guy who'd made a fortune manufacturing pipes or water tanks. They were on the brink of divorce. Sylvia called the husband, who immediately bought the apartment and then not only asked her to sell his house but to find a place for his ex-wife to live as well.

"I did it!" Sylvia boasted on the phone.

"What? I can't hear you," Gaby said. "I've got a bad connection. I'll call you from the lobby."

Sylvia invited her to celebrate at Champs-Élysées. Gaby didn't want to go, but she couldn't come up with a reason to turn it down, apart from the traffic, not wanting to spend money, and not having anything herself to celebrate.

An older woman with a surly expression greeted her at the door, behaving more like a guard than a hostess. Gaby could not understand why her friend subjected herself to such humiliation. Why eat in such a place and not at one of the many restaurants that welcomed them? She went up the spiral staircase. Framed by silk curtains, the spacious restaurant's tall windows looked out on Avenida Reforma. The view, without the street-level noise or people, transformed Reforma. Only the treetops were visible, and they were green rather than dusty like down on the street. The Angel of Independence beamed benevolently over the city as though everything in it were luxurious.

"This is how Europe must look," Gaby said to her friend, who was waiting at the table.

"Why don't we go and see for ourselves?"

"See what?"

"Europe."

"How do you imagine we'd make that happen?"

"Why not, Gaby, why not? Think about it. It's not a matter of money. If you set out to do it, you'll do it. No one relies on you anymore, right? You have to set goals for yourself. If you don't know where you want to go, how will you ever get there? Don't you have an apartment in Palmas, and didn't you get your daughter through one of the best schools in Mexico? You helped her get ahead. But since then you haven't accomplished anything else. She who does not move forward stagnates, my friend; she stagnates."

Gaby was not in the mood to be lectured. The apartment in Palmas had been Sylvia's idea. She'd convinced Gaby that in order to give Adriana a dignified life, she also had to give her class. The plan had failed. Her daughter was a hippie, and Gaby felt like she was getting nowhere fast. Still, she liked the idea of seeing Europe.

Gaby did not know what to order, because the menu, on top of being expensive, seemed foreign to her. She decided on fettuccine with morels. She liked the dish so much that she vowed to duplicate the recipe at home no matter the cost of the mushrooms or how much butter was involved. During the meal the two friends planned their European adventure. Gaby was taking her last sip of coffee when she saw the perfectly draped, dark-blue pants with gray pinstripes. A pair of new-looking black shoes approached the table. It was Don Pedro de León.

"May I buy you ladies a drink?" he asked.

When the waiter brought him a chair, Don Pedro requested a particular bottle of wine. The restaurant was nearly empty, with only a few guests engaged in after-lunch conversation.

"It's a Chilean wine that is quite good," he said, sitting down. "How are you . . . ?"

"Gaby."

"Yes, Gaby, of course. We met at the exhibit, right?" At first he seemed unsure, but then he recovered. "You two were together. She told you that we used to work together. Isn't that right, Sylvia?"

"Yes, Don Pedro."

"Don't call me Don Pedro. I'm not a bottle of brandy. Besides, we're the same age."

Sylvia later told Gaby *that* was the moment she realized that Don Pedro was flirting. In the three years Sylvia had worked for him more than ten years ago, it had never bothered him to be referred to as Don Pedro.

"Really?" asked Gaby, feeling clueless for not having realized it herself. After her first husband left, her friends had said, "Thank God you're finally rid of that drunk." (Her *first* husband; she'd always referred to him simply as her husband, certain that he would be the only one.) But she'd neither gotten rid of him nor realized that he was a drunk. Sure, Pablo drank the way all men drink. At least that's what she had believed.

It turned out that the bottle of wine Don Pedro de León had treated them to was not very good. Months later, after making love, Pedro told Gaby this was the reason he'd started to like her. She'd been content with wine that wasn't all that good, while his wife was never satisfied.

19

The Whore

He had never been a breast man. Pedro much preferred a nice ass and a pair of pretty eyes. Undoubtedly, his main sexual fantasy, the one he'd harbored from the time he was a young boy, was a blow job. That's what he requested from the whore at Rouge, a brothel in the Zona Rosa frequented by his cousins. He wanted to remain a virgin for Marti, who was already his fiancée. Even though he was only sixteen and two years older than her. Of course, she was not his official fiancée, and she would not be until he graduated from college with a degree in business, but for all intents and purposes he was already engaged.

Marti and he had long discussions about sex. Their conversations basically came down to this:

1. They would not have sex until they were married.
2. Once married they would have lots of sex.

Truth be told, the whore frightened him. He had no desire to stick it inside her, so suggesting a blow job seemed like a perfect alternative.

The act itself was delicious, and Pedro grew reckless when he felt he was about to come, demanding, "Swallow, you whore, swallow!"

She gazed up at him, on her knees, with a look of ecstasy or perhaps pleading. Pedro could not figure out her expression. He grabbed her by the hair and yanked her closer. He was not himself. He was beside himself. He wanted to keep it going, to smack her perky ass, nicely framed by a thong and garters. He wanted to rip off her thong and ram it down farther. But he didn't. His heartbeat returned to its normal rhythm, and the whore stopped what she'd been doing. She washed out her mouth and said, "Your little stunt is going to cost you dearly."

"I've got money to spare."

For six months Pedro couldn't stop thinking about that blow job. He'd masturbate thinking about it. He'd stroll near Rouge thinking about it. He started running long distances so as not to think about it. He wanted it, he desired it so much, but he did not return. His impulses scared him.

Finally, he confessed to Father Miguel. Among the guys at school, Father Miguel, who was also their soccer coach, was the most respected confidant for questions related to sex. He'd set up more than one guy with an escort because he was of the savvy opinion that if you could not contain sin, you could at least choose the lesser evil. If his students, the future leaders of Mexico, had to fornicate, they should at least do so with discreet young women of quality—not with brothel whores and, above all, not with their girlfriends, decent señoritas from their sister school and the future mothers of Mexico's leaders.

One day the priest took them to a soccer game, and he introduced Pedro to Marisol. He instructed Pedro to request Marisol's phone number and ask her out to dinner.

"She's not a whore," Father Miguel had warned him, "but she's no señorita. Take her to dinner, flirt with her, and after a few dates, a stroll, or some little trinket you buy her, she'll be happy."

He asked Marisol out to dinner. Pedro was taken aback by how quickly the city divided into two worlds: that of the well-heeled, decent folks—the world Marti knew—and the other city. They did not always have simple boundaries. A restaurant where he'd take Marisol might be next door to one where he'd go with Marti or his parents. But the city was set up in such a way that the two worlds did not collide. Once upon a time he'd had no need for such maps and codes. But now that he was setting out to live a double life, the map presented itself with crystal clarity. It was as though he'd discovered the Rosetta Stone for deciphering codes that he'd learned as a little boy and had kept hidden inside all this time.

20

The Hostess

He agreed to meet Marisol at La Fonda del Refugio. He'd gone there a few times with his grandparents when *chiles en nogada* were in season, but he knew that now, in January, it was a safe place to take her. Who was going to be in the Zona Rosa on a Wednesday afternoon? Besides, the restaurant had small private rooms that made an awkward encounter even more unlikely.

Marisol was already waiting when Pedro arrived two minutes late.

"I thought you weren't coming," she said.

"I'm not even late. It just took me a while to park the car."

"You have a car?"

"Yes."

His parents had bought it for him when he turned sixteen. His mother had hidden the keys in a quesadilla at breakfast. He'd almost lost a tooth when he bit into them. "This way you can take Marti for a ride," his father had said.

On Tuesdays and Thursdays he visited Marti in his new car, but he didn't take her for a ride. Marti was not allowed to be in the car with him. They could only be together at her house, always within a chaperone's field of vision. On weekends they could go out together with friends "as couples" to parties or the movies.

But he wasn't with Marti now; he was with Marisol, and she could go for a ride.

"We can go for a ride after lunch if you'd like."

"I'd love to."

They ate pork *chicharrón en salsa verde* and two chicken breasts in *mole poblano*. Pedro had never seen anyone eat with such relish. Marisol's pleasure in every mouthful was evident in her big eyes. They stood out on her face, which otherwise had no distinguishing features save some baby fat that made her look girlish. Her lips were fleshy and smashed like a flat tire. She looked like a good girl when she smiled, like someone with a good heart. Her face reminded Pedro of an apple, but it also had a fishlike quality, as though her eyes were set too wide.

Marisol's appearance was clean and fresh. Pedro could imagine her in uniform, ironing her shirts for school. Today she was wearing a brown skirt and a pink cotton blouse. She'd evidently made an effort to shine her shoes, but they still looked worn. She worked as a hostess on weekends because the pay was good and the schedule allowed her to stay in school. She was majoring in biology at the Universidad Nacional Autónoma de México. Her dream was to open her own laboratory. She thought it a good business decision, since people always needed blood work done.

"I have a little brother. Sometimes I babysit him. If we keep seeing each other," she said, "we can bring him along for a car ride one of these days. He'd love that."

While paying the bill with the gasoline money his father had given him, Pedro wondered if it was too soon to kiss Marisol.

"How many boyfriends have you had?" he asked her.

"One. We went out for two years, but it ended when he moved to Puebla for work."

"For work? How old was he?"

"Twenty-five."

"And you are?"

"Twenty."

"And you?"

"I just turned eighteen," Pedro lied, adding two years to his age. "You don't mind that I'm younger, do you?"

Pedro took her hand as they left the restaurant. He led her through a crafts market out front, where they sold silver bracelets and earrings. Without saying a word, Pedro picked out a small bracelet and put it on her wrist.

"Do you like it?"

"Yes."

"A lot?"

"Yes. I love that it has the same design as the friezes in Mitla."

"What?"

"There's an archaeological site in Oaxaca called Mitla. That's where this pattern comes from. See? It's like a staircase."

"Would you prefer this one?" he asked, pointing to one twice the width.

"No, no thanks."

He paid the merchant and, feeling very gallant, walked her to his car. It was a white Mustang with gray leather seats. He opened the door for her.

"Where would you like to go?"

"It doesn't matter—just drive."

They drove the length of Avenida de los Insurgentes holding hands. Pedro had never driven so deep into the city, and it made him anxious. Marisol explained that she lived near the Universidad Nacional by Avenida Cuauhtémoc, but that he didn't need to take her that far. She could get a minibus on any corner.

Pedro decided not to take Marisol to her house. He already had home visits with Marti to deal with. What he wanted was a girlfriend to kiss. He turned onto a small, quiet street. He stopped the car and right there went for her lips. The kisses were wet and eager. Pedro felt his breath quickening to match hers. Desire. Saliva. Tongues. He jumped out of his seat and got on top of her. He was already hard—rock hard— but all he wanted was to go on kissing her and feel her body beneath him. He paused for a moment to unbutton her blouse, but Marisol stopped him.

"No, Pedro. Not here, and not in broad daylight."

"I thought you liked it."

"I do."

"So?"

"Let's go someplace else," she said, "where there won't be any people."

"But there's no one here," Pedro said, motioning to the empty street. The sky was the color of cement, with big black clouds threatening rain. "Besides, it's going to rain."

"Okay, but if it rains you have to take me home."

"Fine, but today will be the exception to the rule. You live way out in the middle of nowhere, and I don't want you thinking that I'll go there every day to pick you up and drop you off."

"No."

"Promise?" asked Pedro.

"Yes, I promise."

There was something about Marisol that delighted him. Not just the promise of lots of kisses and fondling. Not just her big eyes. He felt free with her, like he could do whatever he wanted.

Pedro was still between her legs. He grabbed Marisol by the waist so their hips met as they continued kissing. It was a *mole* kiss. It was a *café* kiss. A long kiss. Marisol wrapped her arms around him and caressed his hair until he felt electric shocks along his spine, as though the thunder were crashing over him.

It started raining and hailing. Raindrops the size of cherries pelted the windshield. Pedro felt sheltered inside the car, but he was also a bit nervous about the paint job. He felt Marisol's hands on his dick.

"You're hard."

"Yeah."

"Do you want me to?"

"Yes."

She started fondling it softly with both hands. She held it firmly and delicately at the same time. She knew what she was doing. He came in under a minute.

"Sorry."

"No, no, it doesn't matter."

"It's just that I didn't want you to get dirty."

"Don't worry about it. You'll see. Little by little you'll learn to hold back."

"It's just that I like you a lot."

"Really?"

"Yeah."

He kissed her again. He didn't feel shame, only that he wanted to see her more.

He took her home: three buildings housing hundreds of apartments. He didn't ask which one was hers.

"When will I see you?" he asked.

"Call me whenever you like."

"No, better that we make it a date. On Mondays and Wednesdays, you're mine, okay? From midday until night."

"Unless I'm in the middle of exam week. If I have exams, I'll need to study."

"Okay, except during exam week, but don't get too studious on me, eh?"

21

The Scribes

For two years they met almost every Monday and Wednesday. They'd start the afternoon at a restaurant and then go for a *paseo*. Pedro bought her new shoes when he went to the United States.

One afternoon Pedro, Marisol, and her brother were in front of the church of Santo Domingo, sitting by a fountain and enjoying the fresh breeze. A few vendors were offering the seemingly obsolete trade of being a scribe. They used old typewriters to transcribe what their illiterate clients dictated. Sticking to ready-made phrases and archaic flourishes, the scribes informed someone's sister that they were well, announced the birth of a child, and told of a mother's death.

Pedro left the two sitting at the edge of the fountain. It was a clear day. Marisol had bought Miguel ice cream, and they were sharing it. Pedro enjoyed going on *paseos* with them. They always seemed happy. If it rained, they'd say, "What a downpour!" as though it were the first time they'd felt water. They'd even stick out their tongues to taste the drops. They seemed to go through life carefree, always grateful when he picked them up in the car or treated them to a meal. Pedro did it with pleasure. Marisol was his secret and his hope. It was as though he could still believe in Santa Claus, in something magical whose sole purpose was to make him happy.

The rest of the time Pedro lived in anguish. He was tired. Tired of not knowing what he wanted. Tired of not knowing how to ask for it. Back then, since he understood little about himself or about others, he did—or believed he did—what others expected him to do. Pedro moved along obediently, as though carried by a current that he could barely name. It was a feminine current—that much he knew.

His mother lay in wait every day. "Where's my kiss?" she'd ask as soon as she saw him in the morning. "Have you eaten breakfast? Would you like them to make you something?" When she said, "Look at how long your hair's gotten," Pedro knew that he needed to visit a barber, not in the next couple of days but on that very one. "Where did you find that shirt?" meant "Don't ever wear that again."

She completely controlled him with a careful concoction of kisses, caresses, and insinuations. His mother accounted for every moment and every movement. She and Marti divided Pedro's time between them— except for his Mondays and Wednesdays with Marisol. On those days he ran around the city in his not-so-new Mustang. His mother insinu- ated that they'd buy him another car once he graduated and that they had arranged a job for him with a friend of his father.

Pedro claimed to be studying on Mondays and Wednesdays. It made him laugh that both Marti and his mother were stupid enough to believe him. He'd never cracked open a notebook in his life, and he didn't plan to. He'd learned to work the system from the priests at school. By hook or by crook, they got their hands on every exam. Everything had a price; it was just a matter of arriving at it. If a teacher proved to have integrity, they'd invite him out for a night of drinking and whoring until they gained his confidence. If a teacher was nasty, they'd steal it from him—the university janitors were experts at prying open office doors and desk drawers. The rest of them—the majority of them—they simply paid off. Pedro had no qualms about this. Weren't they supposed to learn how things were run? This was how things were run in Mexico. From the head of state to the bleakest migrant laborer, everyone worked the system. He who did not work the system did not get ahead. That's how it was. And everyone knew it, except a few idealistic dreamers, like his mother and Marti, who still believed in studying and hard work. Although it was possible they did know it. They were not stupid, so perhaps they preferred to ignore the obvious. He had no doubt that his father knew. Each Monday morning Pedro noted his father's wide grin of complicity that implied, *Today you're getting laid.*

Sure enough, today he had gotten laid at Marisol's before heading out for their *paseo.* Marisol's bedroom was still decorated like a little girl's room. Pedro found it delicious to do it between her pink sheets that smelled of fabric softener. He felt wonderful lying naked beside her smooth skin, nearly hairless legs, and dark, round breasts. Sometimes after making love he'd fall asleep. She'd watch him quietly while tenderly caressing his hair for a few moments that seemed eternal. When he'd open his eyes, a poster of his namesake, Pedro Infante, stared at him knowingly. There was never anyone in Marisol's house except Miguel, and he kept busy devouring books while they "chatted" about grown-up things.

Marisol was an easy, grateful lover and—though it hurt Pedro to admit this—an expert one as well. She taught him many things. She explained that it was better not to do it the same way each time but to change things up in order to keep it feeling new. He learned to hold back, to enjoy the moment without getting ahead of himself, knowing that the climax was there waiting. Since Marisol was a biology student, she also understood the technical aspects of sex. Four years after 1968, Marisol was the only woman Pedro knew who'd taken charge of her sexuality.

"By taking the Pill," she'd said, "there's no need for you to pull out or other silliness. Do you want me to get pregnant?"

"No."

"That's what I thought. I don't want to either. With the Pill we won't have any problems."

Now, there in the shadow of the church, Pedro went toward the scribe.

"I want a letter," he said.

"What would you like it to say?"

"That I love her."

"Do you want to propose marriage?"

"No. No, only to say that I love her."

"Don't worry, young man. I'll write you a real beauty," the scribe replied.

> *March 8, 1972*
> *My eternally sweet and faithful beloved,*
> *Words pale beside the raging love I feel for you. Void of*
> *your caresses, my heart knows not how to beat. I die,*
> *because I do not die. You are my sole happiness. I want*
> *to be within you, to feel your heart beating within my*
> *hands.*
> > *Eternally yours,*

"Your name?"

"Pedro."

Quickly, the man completed the letter on thin, pale-blue paper.

"I made you a copy so you won't forget the lovely words you wrote. Would you like to have it?"

Pedro paid him and folded both letters. He walked back to the fountain. He'd never told Marisol that he loved her. But oh how he loved her, and on this perfect day he wanted her to know it.

"Will you lend her to me for a while?" he asked Miguel.

"Okay, but don't take too long. Remember the movie begins at five," he said, smiling much like his sister.

Pedro held Marisol's hand and took her to one of those centuries-old columns. He kissed her (resolving never to forget it) and handed her the letter.

Marisol cracked up while reading it. Pedro, who hadn't been sure what to expect, felt relieved. He hadn't betrayed anyone. It hadn't been a real declaration of love. It was a joke—that was all—a romantic prank.

22
The Traffic

How do you cope with loss? How do you learn to live with what you no longer have? Marta was trying to figure that out. She'd called for a meeting with the trusteeship. Israel, her mother's driver, was trying to get her to the lawyer's office, but they were stuck in traffic. He'd worked for her for fifteen years. Marta had always had her own drivers, but none, other than Baltasar, lasted even a year. They would tire of waiting outside a disco until five in the morning only to discover that she'd left without telling them. When Marti died, it seemed only logical that Israel remain on staff. But Marta could not look at him without thinking of her mother. She would have fired him immediately if she hadn't realized that everything reminded her of her mother.

If there was traffic—and when wasn't there?—Marta would hear her mother's voice calming her, telling her as she always had, "Don't concern yourself over things you can't control." It was like a piece of advice from a self-help book: don't concern yourself over what you can't control. It implied that you should focus on what you could change. Her mother habitually took advantage of the traffic to talk on the phone, do her accounting, plan her week, update her agenda, or even take a siesta.

Marta understood the absurdity of her anger. There was traffic, and nothing she did would change that fact. But the traffic was making them late. She lit one cigarette after another. She felt thirsty, then hot or cold. There was traffic, and she could do absolutely nothing to mitigate her anger. The thought that she might actually be able to put an end to her rage made her even angrier, as though she were trapped in a labyrinth and could not find the exit. Marta boiled over to the point where she stepped out of the car, intending to walk to her destination in high heels, only to realize the futility of her action. She heard her mother's voice and managed to calm herself. She'd started to learn that if she changed what she could, rather than fighting against invincible forces, she felt more in control and consequently somewhat at peace.

I can't change my mother's death, she thought. But perhaps she could influence how it affected her. She couldn't change the fact that she missed her mother so badly, but perhaps if she accepted this as well, if she resigned herself to seeing her everywhere, perhaps she'd feel less bad. She could not undo her father's betrayal. He was already married to Gaby. But she could get back at him. Thanks to her mother's savvy, Marta could take away his money and watch that mollusk of his find a different rock to cling to. She could bring the same misery on him that he'd brought on her. Marta envisioned a bomb, the type that sends shrapnel into every hidden nook, ensuring the explosion is complete and absolute.

If only she'd listened to her mother, or at least the teachers at Ibero. Instead, she'd spent four years cheating, cutting classes, showing up hungover, getting her hands on tests, and bribing and seducing instructors. How was she supposed to manage the business? Her mother had dismissed Manuel and put in a new administrator, but was he trustworthy? Who would be in charge now? Her? Could she let the trusteeship handle everything, or did she need to show her face from time to time?

Her summer internships at the company had proved disastrous. She couldn't find anything she enjoyed doing: neither collecting rent, nor overseeing construction, nor scoping out lots. Finally, they'd sent her along with the real estate agents to show apartments, but Marta drank coffee and talked on the phone while the agents showed clients around the properties. She considered it very much beneath her to parade about discussing the number of bedrooms and bathrooms.

The car finally arrived at the offices of Órnelas de Montesinos, inside the building known as El Pantalón because of its pants-like shape.

"Does my father contribute anything to the business?" Marta asked the council after apologizing for being late.

"No," came the unanimous reply.

"Is his salary market rate, or could someone else do the same work for less?"

"The same for less," they replied.

"Therefore it's in the best interest of the company to replace him with someone else. Are we all in agreement?" she said in a confident tone.

"Are you certain?" asked Juan Órnelas de Montesinos. The lawyer hadn't fully sized up his new client. She was very different from her mother.

"Who will advise Pedro of the decision?" asked Father Patrick.

"I will," said Marta with certainty.

The next day Marta went to see her father at his office. She greeted all the secretaries, whom she'd known since childhood and who had so loved her mother.

"Dad, I don't want you to work for us any longer."

"Why?" Pedro was genuinely surprised.

("I saw that coming," Gaby said to him when he gave her the news. "It's obvious that she wants to leave us penniless.")

"I honestly don't think Mom would have approved of your relationship with that servant," Marta said.

She'd wanted to ask him about the other lowlife he'd had—the one they said was her mother, the one with the laboratories—but she didn't dare. Marta wanted to remind him that neither she nor her mother had minded paying for his whores, that they'd always been willing to support his habit. But there was a limit to how much she could humiliate someone on a given occasion. She turned around and walked out of the office.

Marta had intended to hurt her father. From her point of view, she was only doing what was fair: an eye for an eye. She had no desire to abuse her position. He had chosen to abandon her, and she had no choice but to do the same and abandon him.

Before leaving, she'd said, "I'll start coming by the office on Monday. Please take your things."

Pedro wished he had known better. Did he know this might happen when he married Gaby? Why? He couldn't stop asking himself. He never suspected Marta capable of such behavior. He'd thought she'd get angry and that would be the end of it. His daughter had never acted against him. He didn't know what to do. He'd always thought that everything he had was his. Not for a second had he imagined that someone could take it away from him.

Pedro recalled the second time he ran the New York City Marathon. He crossed the finish line five minutes faster than his best time. He was feeling ecstatic. Suddenly, the terrible stomach discomfort he'd been battling for almost three hours got much worse. Doubled over in pain, he entered the first porta-potty he could find. He vomited so badly that it wasn't until afterward that he noticed the filth and stink. He got out, only to vomit again on his shoes. Disgusted and supremely self-conscious, he sat under a tree, trying to go unseen, all the while wishing someone would notice him and help. He thought that he might die. Now he remembered that moment with horror.

He never told anyone. He was unable to articulate it. His friends admired him for having greatly improved his running time, a not insignificant achievement. But he was unable to enjoy his triumph. Whenever he ran a marathon after that, he'd experience a similar panic (although he never again vomited), which grew worse until he stopped running. His body never failed him again. Until now that is; now he was trembling with fury.

Marti had allowed him to believe that he held the reins, but she'd been mocking him the whole time. Pedro grabbed the Tums from his desk drawer. He'd been suffering from unbearable heartburn ever since Marta announced that she was selling Villa del Mar.

23

The Diet

Marta awoke feeling pensive, still wrapped in her dreams. She was hungry, thinking about childhood morning meals with her mother. They would eat in the breakfast nook, which was filled with sunlight from the garden. It was a cozy spot with a round table in the middle, and a collection of porcelain on the wall. The centerpiece was always a silver planter with ivy, flowers from their garden, or remnants from one of the many bouquets her mother received.

Breakfast was inevitably splendid. Since her mother only had coffee and toast and her father ate at the country club, the cook channeled all her efforts into pleasing Marta. She made waffles, hot cakes, *tamales*, muffins, enchiladas, *chilaquiles*, pozole, scrambled eggs, quesadillas, nopales, mushrooms, juice and fruit, beans, eggs sunny-side up or *ranchero*, *sopes*, torpedo-shaped *tlacoyos* made of masa, potato tacos, *machaca* of crushed dried meat with eggs, and scrambled eggs with chorizo.

Marta mouthed the name of each dish as though reciting a poem by heart, a litany or a prayer for something from long ago. It had been years since she'd eaten such things.

Those breakfasts were happy moments. Later, the only thing Marta could recall was how her mother watched her eat, attempting to hide the anxiety that gnawed away at her, assessing every bite with horror, counting every calorie. Marta understood; she'd seen the hips that provoked her mother's anguish. Her mother feared—and eventually she passed on this dread to Marta—that if her daughter kept eating with such gusto, she would start to fill out with the same common curves of her biological mother.

For that reason Marta accepted the disappearance of Gansito cakes and other snacks from her daily diet. She accepted the prohibition against eating between meals. First she gave up tortillas and then cheese. Then the cook became expert at preparing light dishes made with yogurt instead of cream. Next, baked nopales took the place of bread, eggs were poached, and fruit was served without honey or granola.

No one likes a fat girl. Marti never regretted what she'd done. Not even when she realized that Marta barely ate. *Better a little less than a little more,* Marti thought. When Marta's growth spurt hit and Marti had to look up at the girl, she felt proud. She was so beautiful, thin, delicate, and well proportioned.

For her part, Marta resigned herself to the situation the way one accepts walking into a shower with no hot water. She'd allowed her mother to love her as an object. That was it. To Marti she was just another object, like a house, a car, or a painting. However, Marta was her most precious object. Marti had never been able to perceive her as a person. It had taken Marta a long time to grasp this. It was comforting to realize that Marti was incapable of seeing anyone as a person; she only identified with objects.

Marta, now more awake, asked for coffee over the intercom and turned on her computer. Nine o'clock. Too early to find Adriana. Marta didn't know why she felt that it was important to tell Adriana about ousting her father from the job he thought he'd have forever. It was stupid; it only affected Adriana indirectly.

Adriana was very free. She traipsed about the world working on her projects. Marta would like to do something similar, but what? Now she would have an office. What was she going to do with all that?

She picked up the intercom receiver and spoke with the kitchen again.

"Bring me up some *chilaquiles*, please, with everything on them."

24

The Laugh

It was a day like any other. At least Marti couldn't remember anything that made it stand out until the moment she decided to laugh. She'd felt so sad, so weary of herself and her tears, of the desperation. She was exhausted.

She greeted someone and made it a point to smile. Perhaps she smiled too much—it was a fake gesture to mask her feelings. She painfully remembered her mother digging her nails into her arm while whispering, "Smile, smile."

That's how she'd been brought up. The gesture became automatic:

Pinch = smile.

Pain = smile.

This day, after all of these years, she decided to broaden her upbringing:

Sadness = smile.

And she burst out laughing.

She practiced laughing in a way that flowed well, observing precisely when it was used to best effect. She did not want to come off as demented. She wanted more than anything to pass for a normal, happy person.

She started doing it after people would ask, "How are you?" She'd look the person in the eye, let out a small burst of laughter, barely more than a smile, and then answer, "Great. And you?"

When possible she'd hold the person's hand so that even a trivial conversation would seem more personal and warm. Slowly, she learned to kid around, with little jokes preceding her laugh. So as not to offend anyone, she directed the jokes at herself. She frequently ended her statements with "I'm so silly!" (laugh); "I'm such an idiot!" (laugh); "I'm so absentminded!" (laugh); "There I go again!" (laugh). People seemed to like it. It made them feel at ease and allowed them to open up to her.

"She has a wonderful sense of humor," they'd say. "She's always so cheerful, so *simpática*."

Before long she was doing it without thinking. It evolved into something authentic. It became second nature. But in truth she never forgot her upbringing: pain = smile; sadness or anguish = smile. So it was understandable that she would enter the surgeon's office laughing, determined to keep doing so until her death.

25

Morelianas

When would this absurd inner dialogue with her mother finally end? The only upside to the mess in Marta's head was that it had pushed out the incessant anguish over her weight that she had carried around since she was a little girl. Years of counting calories, self-control, and punishments no longer had a place in her head. She could not remember what she had eaten for breakfast. Nowadays she ate only when she was hungry, never giving a second thought to food. Once, she could have spent an entire day thinking about a piece of cake she'd eaten three days ago, then drink water nonstop to flush it from her system while counting the minutes until evening, when she'd snort some cocaine to feel good again.

Right now, riding in the car, she felt hungry. "Call over that vendor," she told the driver as they stopped for a traffic light. "What is he selling, Israel?"

"Morelianas."

"Do you have change? Buy a few from him, please."

With a piercing whistle, he called over the man carrying a cardboard box with packages of caramel cookies wrapped in clear plastic. Marta watched the man from the window of her armored van. Someone was selling something at every traffic light in the city. You could buy water, cords for your cell phone, toys, sweets, cigarettes, calling cards; even handcrafted goods competed with the latest black-market items from China. Every house in Mexico had some item from this trade: the fifteen-piece Tupperware set bought for forty pesos that would cost two hundred in the supermarket; the plastic penguin-shaped garbage bin; the miniature guitar with four strings that you could never tune; and countless peanuts, wafers, popsicle sticks, gum, and newspapers.

Israel handed Marta the *morelianas* and hit the gas, leaving the vendor in the dust. She could not remember the last time she'd eaten these, but her memory anticipated their sweetness. She undid the simple fold of the plastic wrapper. Eight brown rounds of caramel scattered their sugary scent throughout the car. She bit into one. It was crunchy, but as it warmed in her mouth, it melted into a sweet and delicious cream. She ate the rest of the cookie in a single bite. She wolfed them down one after another. She didn't feel a cloying sensation or the need for water. Quite the contrary: she felt almost happy. She felt full, a sensation she had not experienced in a long, long time. The last remnants of flavor were encrusted between her molars.

"Why don't we ever buy *morelianas*, Israel, when they're so good?"

He shrugged his shoulders.

At that moment her cell phone rang. It was Mau.

Marta searched for her pack of Marlboro reds, wanting to light a cigarette the way she always did when she talked on the phone. Instead, she opened the window and threw out the pack. She had an urge to start giving in to her impulses. She breathed in deeply before speaking, as though she had inhaled smoke.

"She called you? . . . Why not me? . . . What? . . . Should we go? . . . No, no one comes to mind . . . You? . . . If you want, I'll call him . . . I'll let you know ASAP . . . Great . . . I'll dial it now . . . Right . . . Bye."

Marta wondered why Adriana had called Mauricio and not her. On the beach trip she'd felt they'd started a potentially important friendship. Using her index finger, she deftly ran through her cell phone's contacts. When she located the one she wanted, she clicked on it and pressed "Call."

"Manolo, hi . . . Yes . . . Are you busy? . . . Call me back, okay? . . . Thanks . . . Yes, use this number."

Her nails glided over the tiny keyboard as she texted Mau: *OK, will call me back soon.*

Fifteen minutes later, when traffic finally started to unravel and they were moving along the Periférico toward Reforma, Marta's phone rang.

"Hi, how are you? . . . Yes, I got back two days ago . . . How did you know? . . . Yes, it's too much house for me. Too many memories . . . Yes . . . Well, we want to go to New York, and I remembered that you fly there all the time. So you're going? . . . Can you take us? . . . Just Mau and me. You'll let me know? . . . Thanks."

She hung up and quickly texted Mau: *Got plane.* Then she called him.

"He has a meeting on Thursday. When he's finished he'll call us, and we can meet him at the airport in Toluca. Done."

The smell of roasted chili peppers cooking on a hot plate filled the street. Marta closed the window and asked Israel to blast the music.

26

The Sheep

Adriana's first few days in New York were a whirlwind: setting up the Lower East Side apartment that the gallery rep had loaned her; relearning how to use the subway; waiting for the art to arrive; renegotiating her contract with Larry Stein. Nothing was particularly difficult, but everything required effort, from activating a local cell phone to getting used to the food. But what really wore her out was seeing. Seeing! In Mexico she had more or less seen it all, and her gaze would fix on something that stood out, something unusual, which was not infrequent. But in New York everything was new: all the people—all the different types of people—the street signs, and the store windows. She wanted to see and memorize it all. The city changed at a dizzying rate. Having visited before did not make her feel any less a foreigner. English bounced around her head like a basketball.

She'd asked Larry if she could remain in New York for two months after her show opened in order to work on a new project. Although she felt dazed by the city, Adriana realized that she needed to concentrate, to keep up, or else she'd never complete it. Besides, she was determined to disprove her dealer's skepticism.

She had been turning the idea around for months. But when she explained it to Larry, he was not impressed. However, she didn't let up. Adriana knew that he could not envision the final product, and that she'd have to present a nearly finished work for him to appreciate her concept.

Her idea for making nativity scenes seemed old-fashioned and generic to him. But what she wanted was precisely to renew the cliché. She sought to create contemporary nativities so that people would see them with fresh eyes, so they'd ask themselves about the implications of God making man in his image. Over time artists had depicted Jesus and the Virgin according to their era. In the Middle Ages there were wooden cribs, humble mangers, the swaddled Child, the Virgin wearing stiff veils that covered her face. In the Renaissance they did it according to the visions of Saint Bridget of Sweden, which had been translated into Latin and described the Child illuminated and nude, the blond Virgin kneeling, and the angels singing.

It wasn't only that each era's painters learned new techniques; rather, they had different ways of seeing life and consequently the birth of Christ. People had always seen a Mary and a Joseph who represented them as they were in their own contemporary time. Even the nativities of the Conquista had needed to take on indigenous features in order to be accepted. When the first missionaries reached Japan, they made Christ with slanted eyes. Why not now? Nativity scenes had existed from the first century. Saint Francis of Assisi came up with the idea of creating the first human representation of the nativity and had to ask permission from Pope Honorius III.

Influenced by the dramatizations of nativity scenes she'd seen as a child and the classic paintings she admired as an adult, Adriana wanted to portray men and women with their babies, the way they dressed daily, naturally, in jeans and skirts. She sought to cast a wide net of modern parents, from married gay couples and punk couples, to immigrants of all nationalities. The photos would be large format, mounted in polished aluminum frames and perhaps even lit from behind like spectacular billboards. They needed to be colorful and gleaming.

After scouting the city for a good location, she decided that Sheep Meadow in Central Park would be the best place to find all sorts of families with young children. She hoped Larry would help her get the necessary permits from the city and that his three assistants would help with the staging, finding the families, and obtaining the signed releases.

"I need a donkey, two sheep, and a cow," she told Larry.

"Live?"

"They have to be. They're in all the nativities. I can't do it without them. They're essential elements."

"I think it'll be difficult."

"Ask."

"They're not going to lend them to us."

"Ask! If they say no, I'll see what else I can do, but I need you to really try, okay, Larry? I'm telling you that I need them. This is the project that will establish me as an artist."

"You're already established."

"Larry, how much are my pieces selling for?"

"Twenty thousand."

"Well, if you'd like them to sell for two hundred thousand someday, get me the animals."

With Larry it was better to discuss matters in financial terms rather than artistic ones, even if he would have sworn to the contrary.

Stretched out on her futon, which she'd set up near the window to get some air and enjoy the view, dressed only in a T-shirt and black underwear, Adriana was on the phone with Marta.

"I can't believe he doesn't see it, that he doesn't understand that I must have the animals."

"What will you do if he doesn't obtain the permits?" asked Marta.

"I don't know. Photoshop, I guess. But he better get them. Do you know what this city is capable of doing in the name of art? They shut down entire streets, they build waterfalls, they assemble floating museums. One donkey and one cow are nothing next to that."

"Maybe I can get them for you."

"You?"

"Sure, I know one of the main donors to the zoo."

"The zoo?"

"The Central Park Zoo. I think the person I know donated the entire penguin exhibit."

"I didn't know there was a zoo in the park."

"Right next to Sheep Meadow."

"How do you know this person? Forgive me. Why am I asking? You know everyone. What do I care?"

Adriana marveled at Marta's power and influence. The world was a small place to her. She could simply pick up the phone and get whatever she wanted, be it a plane or donkeys. She carried herself with a sense of entitlement, from the way she boarded the yacht to how it was no big deal knowing people in Milan.

"We met when my mom was on the committee to rescue Bosque de Chapultepec," Marta said. "They served as her advisers."

Since their afternoon on the yacht, Marta called Adriana almost every day. At first it had seemed strange, but soon Adriana accepted it as a pleasant reality and even looked forward to it.

One day without meaning to, she asked, "Why didn't you call me yesterday?"

"I don't know," Marta said. "Why didn't you call me?"

"You always call me."

"You can call me too, you know."

"Yes."

"So why don't you?"

"I don't know."

"Well, then don't complain."

Adriana felt closer to Marta now that she had permission to call her, a privilege she had not thought was hers.

"When do you arrive?"

"Friday."

"Do you want me to come meet you?"

Where had that come from? Adriana had never met anyone at the airport.

"No, thanks. They're picking me up."

Adriana breathed a sigh of relief.

"Let me see if I can get you those donkeys. When do you need them?"

"September fifteenth through thirtieth."

"That's more than a week."

"I know."

"Okay."

Adriana mumbled.

"What did you say?"

"Thanks," Adriana said.

"What?"

"*Thanks!*" Adriana yelled into the receiver.

"Kiss."

"Bye."

Adriana hung up the phone. She felt Marta's kiss on her mouth.

Her mother had reproached her for being friends with Marta. "Don't you see that she hates us, that she wants to destroy us?"

"Mom, that has nothing to do with me," she'd answered. But now Adriana understood what had impressed her mother so much about Pedro's world. Now Adriana wanted to belong to it too. She was determined to ignore anything that got in her way, including her own mother.

27

The Donkey

What was she getting herself into? What did it matter? Marta couldn't remember the last time she'd had this much fun. It certainly was better than the doldrums she'd been mired in since her mother's death.

The trusteeship approved the sale of Villa del Mar, and Marta entertained herself chatting with real estate agents and potential clients. Two Americans were fighting over the property, and if all turned out well it would sell for a 30 percent profit. Perhaps she was not as bad at business as people imagined.

Marta called her personal banker at Citibank. She'd never had any intention of bothering the zoo's adviser, but she did not want to admit to Adriana that she was planning to buy the animals. Years of tutelage by her mother had taught Marta which favors could be requested and which were better avoided. Fortunately, that which could not be requested could almost always be purchased.

"Michael, it's Marta de León Tordella de la Vega. How are you? I need to ask you a favor."

Bankers like Michael existed specifically to grant people like her favors.

"Whatever you need, Marti—sorry, Marta. It's just that you have your mother's voice."

"Everyone tells me that."

"You already have your usual suite reserved. What can I get for you? Tickets?"

"No, no, it's something a bit more unusual."

"You know we're here to serve you. There's nothing I haven't heard before. Believe me."

"I need a cow, a donkey, and two sheep for two weeks in Central Park."

"You want what?"

"I can ask someone else. I know it's a strange request. It's for a work of art."

"Sure, sure, I understand. Let me see what I can do for you."

Renting the animals and their trailer, plus securing the parking permit and two shepherds, cost ten thousand dollars. Marta paid happily. As soon as she'd arranged everything, she heard her mother's voice saying, "Don't expect gratitude." Marta knew how often her mother had been let down after helping someone out.

"When people need help and want something, they're very good at asking for it. But the minute you give them what they need, their pride returns. They'll never thank you. They think they've earned it, that it was owed to them. When you do give, do it without expecting anything in return, because you will receive nothing."

Marta couldn't count the number of times she'd heard variations on that speech. She didn't want to think about what she wanted from Adriana or how she expected Adriana to show her gratitude. She only wanted to help.

28
The Gallery

We r coming. Adriana was in the middle of installing her work when she saw Mauricio's text. She bit her lip involuntarily, her body reacting before her mind knew what to think. She was already on edge about the show. It was always like this—a nearly debilitating sensation gripped her. Normally, she was more than capable of walking and talking, of living, without giving much thought to what she was doing. Now every gesture took effort, every step strained her tendons, and every phrase felt like a battle. When she tried to speak, she turned into a stuttering mute.

The gallery was so pristine that she panicked, feeling ashamed to hang her pictures there. What if they sullied the space? Staring at the smooth white walls, the majestic space, the perfect lighting, Adriana started hyperventilating. The canvases were still boxed up, yet she was already being asked her thoughts on this or that wall. Adriana's art burst with color, so they chose to leave the walls white. Except for the collage of her mother's receipts; they would hang on an intensely dark-blue wall to serve as a foil for the thousands of white and yellow pieces of paper.

The next day the gallery looked like it had been hit by a tornado. There were boxes and packages strewn about the floor, canvases leaning on every wall, and the lights weren't working properly. The space had grown oppressive. Adriana felt like she had to flee. What if her work was not well received? There was already too much garbage in the world. What if her paintings were just more garbage, more duplicated garbage?

She thought about Duchamp's urinal and his bicycle tire on a bench. They were garbage that functioned as inflection points. But they were more than that. They had an aesthetic quality that defied temporality. Was that an intrinsic quality, or did it stem from having defined a certain trend that later became iconic?

Adriana tried to recall the first time she'd seen them displayed in a museum. But no, she'd never really seen them with fresh eyes, just like she could not see her own work that way. There was always a prior photograph, an earlier image.

"What about this wall? Centering the three canvases here would be a bit of a tight squeeze. We could put two and two here, although thematically—"

"No, no, leave the three there," said Adriana, forced to focus, "but put the Facebook one in the center."

If you looked at them closely—and Adriana wondered if anyone would bother—each self-portrait told a story. You could glean so much about people from their Facebook profiles. You got a picture of their face, the photographs they shared, the number of friends they had, whether they were extroverted, their date of birth, their tastes in movies, the places they traveled, and their marital status. In truth, *that* Facebook page no longer existed; her painting of it was not just a portrait, it was also a historical record.

It was akin to looking through a stranger's passport. So many "truths" become instantly accessible: age, place of birth, travel destinations. Yet no one believes that their passport reflects their authentic self. The contents are merely *les chiffres*—facts and figures that interest only adults and which Saint-Exupéry so enjoyed criticizing. How much money do they have? What street do they live on? No one asks about the tone of their voice or what games they like. What did Adriana's paintings say? Were they the voice or *les chiffres*? Could you see a person's soul in her portraits?

Adriana left the gallery as soon as she could. She fled to MoMA in order to calm herself within its walls. It was here, in this museum—on this very patio, she was almost certain—that she had decided to dedicate herself to art. She had been eighteen years old then and bursting with things to say. She'd been flooded with feelings and ideas; she'd seen everything within those walls—beauty, hatred, anguish, disgust, envy, love, respect, passion. She had listened to questions and answers, to conversations that had lasted for centuries. She had wanted to be a part of that.

When she got back to her room at the Paramount Hotel later that night after visiting MoMA for the first time, her boyfriend was watching television. She undressed and pulled off the bedsheet. She wrapped her body like a Greek goddess wearing a cloak and jumped on the sole chair in that tiny room, announcing in a loud voice filled with rapture, "I am going to be an artist."

"You think you'd dig that?"

"Yep, I am going to enroll at San Carlos as soon as we get home. I need to learn how to say everything I want to say."

How she had worked since then! Her mother didn't approve, but in spite of her mother's opposition she had her professors' acceptance, her peers' envy and admiration, and her own determination to sacrifice friendships, relationships, and even sleep. Adriana didn't normally look back. The moment she reached a goal, her mind moved on to the next one.

Last year MoMA had purchased one of her dressing-room photographs. It had not been displayed yet. Adriana knew the woman in charge of new acquisitions, a cautious buyer who preferred to collect a bit of this and a bit of that in order to avoid mistakes. It was a relatively inexpensive market, so when Adriana found out that they'd acquired her photo she was pleased but did not feel like a part of the museum. She wasn't a part of the dialogue. Her voice remained no more than a whisper. She wanted to enter the conversation with a roar. How could she do that? By creating a perspective that the world wanted to see—or did not wish to see but would be obliged to—forming part of the public domain, part of humanity's cultural heritage, like the early art of Louise Bourgeois. *Some whispers are intense,* she thought.

The museum had undergone a complete renovation since the last time Adriana visited. Only the patio retained its former essence; the rest of the museum had been turned into an odd hybrid of luxury storefront and subway station.

We r coming. Her cell phone vibrated again. Shit, she had enough worries without having to think about Mau and Marta. She tried to calm herself. It could be fun to have friends around. Marta could certainly introduce her to interesting people in New York. But Adriana didn't want to enjoy herself too much. She had to establish boundaries if she was to complete her next project.

On the third day Adriana's anxiety turned into anticipation. She was excited. She vacillated between admiring her canvases and hating them. The gallery was transformed by her art. Her paintings made a statement. Moreover, they offered something original, which was the essence of her artistic mission. They were modern and original, yet the oils gave them a luster and a classic quality.

29

The Ring

They nearly always had sex on Mondays, which proved to be a bonus for Pedro: he could put up with the formal couples' outings with Marti on weekends by looking forward to Marisol. Although his relationship with Marti was real and the one with Marisol was woven with lies, it was the latter that seemed more authentic to Pedro, even if he couldn't quite articulate it. He would have preferred that not to be the case. He tried to talk as freely with Marti as he did with Marisol; he really tried, but he couldn't.

He had to tiptoe around Marti, thinking and rethinking his words before opening his mouth. It was easier to remain quiet than to be corrected. How many times had it happened? He'd say something, only to have Marti contradict him: children in Japan *didn't* only attend school until they were seven; there *were* no bicycles two hundred years ago. Or some other drivel. What did it matter what occurred in Japan? Or two hundred years ago? At the movies Marti knew all the actors' names, and she could recall the films that the director, and the director of photography, had made. In the meantime Pedro could barely recall the recent blockbusters. After seeing the films, Marti pestered him with questions about art, philosophy, and politics, all things he didn't know anything about and didn't want to answer. It's not that he minded discussing a movie for a little while, but two hours? Did you like it? Yes? No? Done!

"What else would you like to discuss?" Marti would ask him innocently, wanting to please him.

"Nothing," Pedro would answer, irritated. He wanted to scream *"Nothing!"* but he held back. He wasn't really sure why her questions bothered him so much. He held her hand to pacify her: "We don't always have to speak, do we?"

Pedro and Marti had many things of which to be proud. They often talked about how they were the leaders among their friends and had to set a good example. More than anything they were happy that they'd never broken up, like those couples that ruined their relationships with temporary splits and arguments.

"We're not like that," Marti would say.

"No, not us," Pedro would agree while holding her hand.

"How can you forgive someone who does such things? Just imagine! At Conchita's party, he told her she looked like a maid. How can you forgive such insults?"

"But," said Pedro, thinking of Marisol, "sometimes you need to forgive."

"Yes," added Marti, remembering that one should be charitable. "You need to put yourself in the other person's place, and when you are married you have to forgive everything. Father Patrick says that you have to forgive everything, right?"

"Yes," said Pedro, relaxing a bit, feeling proud and secure in his future wife's upbringing. "You need to forgive everything."

Pedro believed that life as he knew it was coming to an end. In two months he would complete his final exams and graduate with a degree in business administration. He had already purchased a thesis on the construction industry and was preparing his oral defense.

Marti's parents asked him to join them on their trip to Paris, which meant entering a more formal level in their engagement. Pedro's mother insinuated that he needed to buy the ring ahead of time in order to propose to Marti before they returned from France.

While he watched television seated on the living room couch, his parents attempted to include him in the conversation about which restaurant was best suited for the proposal.

"Choose whichever you want," Pedro said, keeping his eyes glued to the screen. "I've never been to Paris. Besides, what does it matter? She'll be the first of her friends with a ring and the only one proposed to in Europe. She'll be happy. She can brag about it for years."

"That's exactly the reason why the location is important," said his mother.

"Precisely," reiterated his father.

"La Tour d'Argent!" his mother decided suddenly. "It has an unforgettable view of Notre-Dame."

He was supposed to spend two months' wages on the ring.

"You have to buy it with your own money," said his father. "It's a question of honor. We'll help out with the rest."

Pedro had a free week between graduation and the trip to Paris. After that he'd start his well-paid job at his uncle's construction firm. He would not be able to see Marisol like before. His uncle was no blockhead. He would have him working from eight in the morning until eight at night. Pedro decided to spend his last week of freedom with Marisol. She was like the gun in that Beatles song, a well-honed pistol that was a pleasure to shoot. "I feel my finger on your trigger," he comforted himself by repeating.

Pedro could not see that his whole future lay ahead of him. On the contrary he drifted like a shipwrecked sailor dragged by the current toward the horizon. He feared that behind the straight line was a precipice, adult life, into which he would fall without a harness.

30

The Store

Following her banker's suggestion, Marta stayed at the Mandarin Oriental in the Time Warner Center. She booked herself in one of the priciest rooms, while Mau reserved the cheapest. He made sure of this by asking three times if they could get him a cheaper room. After settling in, they met in the lobby to go shopping before heading to Adriana's opening. Marta wanted to go to Bergdorf Goodman, and Mau coveted a pair of shoes from Tod's. Marta turned into a voracious predator. She scoured the entire store, filling up an immense fitting room and trying on clothes for almost two hours. Mau waited patiently on a settee, venturing the occasional opinion. Marta bought so much stuff that they had the bags delivered directly to the hotel so they wouldn't have to carry them.

It's my life, thought Marta, *mine and no one else's. It's my life until God or cancer or the fairies take it from me. Until then it's my life, and I'll make of it what I want.*

The anxiety resurfaced as soon as she was done shopping. Marta craved something else—no, she was dying for—a snort, a blunt, a drink, a cigarette, anything to calm her, anything to extinguish the anxiety poking at her like a thousand pinpricks all over her body.

"Mau, you got anything on you?" she asked, feeling pallid.

"No. You want some coffee?"

"Fucking coffee? Can't you come up with something better?"

"How about a drink?"

"Yes."

"At the Four Seasons?"

"Let's go."

They walked along Fifty-Eighth Street to the hotel. Its scale made them feel grand and small at the same time. They sat on the bar's comfortable red leather seats. Marta asked for a martini and then another. She started feeling better. She'd tried on everything that caught her eye and bought half of what she modeled in front of the mirror. Four or five pairs of pants, three or four dresses. How many pairs of shoes? She'd lost count. She had *wanted* everything. She would've sworn that she needed everything. Her mammoth hunger seemed to capsize onto the store. Yet she felt incredibly empty. Shopping had always been a ritual she'd shared with her mother. Well, with her or against her but always alongside her. They'd agree on outfits, admire each other, and share tips while shopping. Marta knew exactly how her mother liked her to dress: black made her look pale; navy blue was elegant; mustard yellow didn't work on her in bright light; gabardine made her eyes stand out. Of course, white always looked good on her. Red required judicious use—never red on the lips; that was only for whores. Clothes had to look polished without advertising their cost. Brands had to be worn inside because it was in bad taste to serve as a designer's billboard. Marta also knew what her mother didn't like. "Don't look men in the eyes . . . You're too old for miniskirts and you should learn to close your legs . . . You look like a punk, like a *puta*, like you're crazy." Still, she'd always been there, someone to look at her: her mother, her mirror.

Her mother's absence made Marta confront something she had never wanted to admit: she'd been a pendulum displaced between two points—between two mothers, one present and the other absent, one biological, the other imposed. She swung from one end to the other. No one could understand how the daughter of Marti Tordella had turned out so rebellious with such an irreproachable mother. But they didn't know the truth. Marta rejected her mother's expectations and pushed the limits as attempts to force Marti to admit that Marta wasn't her daughter. But who was she now? Mau had told her back in Mexico, without realizing what he was saying, that Marta was truly becoming her mother's daughter.

"Mau, a cigarette?"

"You can't smoke in here."

"Right. Ah, shit, okay. On the way out we'll buy some."

Mau took care of the tab, and they left the bar. *Maybe the smoke will help,* thought Marta. She'd gone a week without smoking, but the craving had returned *en force* with the martinis. Cigarettes would solve everything. She could fill up on smoke.

They went into the lobby and found themselves by a restaurant. At the far end of it there was a spit of chickens turning in a high-tech rotisserie. Blond wood paneling marked off the cozy space, which had ceilings that soared over twenty feet. Sliced carrots and cucumbers floated like sculptures inside immense crystal jars filled with water. The restaurant had strategically placed spotlights illuminating each table, lending everything a rich hue right out of a glossy magazine. There was just one couple seated by the window.

"Why don't we eat something?" Marta said suddenly, imagining herself pumped with nutrients instead of smoke. "Are you hungry?"

"I am. Isn't this that famous chef's place?" asked Mau, recognizing Robuchon's name on the menu. "I think he's known for his mashed potatoes."

"What could be so special about mashed potatoes? Of course, now I want some. Let's get an order."

Since it wasn't crowded, they were seated immediately.

"Doesn't this look yummy?" Mau said, studying the menu. "Foie with eel."

"Hmm, what an odd combination. Let's order it. What else to start? Pick something. What about entrées? Some meat? You can't go wrong with Kobe beef and mashed potatoes."

The sommelier recommended a bottle of 1992 Finca Villacreces.

"You're looking better," said Mau after a few seconds of nibbling on bread and butter. "Maybe you were just hungry."

"I'm always hungry now. You know, I never felt hungry before. Well, either I didn't feel it, or I didn't let it bother me. It's odd, but I've started enjoying food recently."

"Well, you certainly look better."

"You've noticed? Why didn't you say something?"

Mau shrugged. Marta had gained weight. It wasn't that she'd gotten heavy exactly, but she'd filled in, softening her angles. She remained a gorgeous example of the skinny bitch, but the pallor and the hint of illness had evaporated.

"Mau, do you remember in Villa del Mar when you said I was starting to seem like my mother's daughter? What were you referring to?" Marta asked while the waiter set down the smoked eel topped with a strip of foie gras. It was plated like a work of modern art, with flecks of brilliant color.

"I don't know," said Mau. "I thought you were finding your destiny. Like your grandmother did with the vaccines and your mom with her maternity clinics. I thought you were finding your place in society by doing something like that, something admirable."

He leaned in to her aqua-green eyes and saw, as he always did, their beauty. He continued to observe Marta while chewing on a piece of foie. He thought he spotted a twinkle in her eyes.

"I feel a void, Mau, such a huge void since my mom . . ."

"Marta, you've told me this already, but what about before your mom? It's not like you were superhappy."

I know, thought Marta as she tried another piece of the dish. The tender eel was smoky and sweet, and the fatty, delicate foie was velvety smooth. Carefully, she put another piece on her fork and placed it on Mau's lips. He hadn't shaved that morning and his mouth, framed with stubble, was seductive.

"So what would you have me do?" asked Marta.

"I don't know, something with cancer or something for anorexics. Or something to do with art. Why did you want to come here?"

"Shopping?" she answered without thinking. She had a way of deflecting conversations when they turned to serious topics. Marta wasn't ready to admit that she felt she might learn something from Adriana. Marta admired her independence and how she came from nothing. She was intrigued by Adriana's utter lack of interest in marriage. She was vastly different from the people Marta knew.

"Mau, how do you explain that Gaby is a low-class *naca* while Adriana is not?"

"In what ways?"

"I don't know, from her way of dressing to how she thinks. Does Adriana seem *naca* to you?"

"No."

"And Gaby?"

"Obviously."

"Okay, but why?"

"Well, in the first place, Adriana has no interest in pretending to be from a different social class. Quite the opposite—she couldn't care less and goes out of her way to stress it by letting you know that she rides the subway and has no money, that sort of thing. Gaby, on the other hand, does everything possible to deny where she came from."

"Adriana is supercultured. Have you noticed how much she knows?"

"Yeah, and it's not like she's even traveled much."

"She's traveled for her exhibits."

"Sure, backpacking and stuff. She told me that she stayed in Europe for three months after the Venice Biennial. But she did it on the cheap, sleeping in train stations and hostels."

"C'mon, dude, what does it matter? You've slept on the street."

"Never."

"Not even drunk?"

"Nope. You?"

"In Acapulco," she said, remembering when she'd woken up in the hallway of an apartment where her friends were staying. The bitches had left her outside.

"I'm not buying it. You wouldn't be here if you'd spent the night on the streets of Acapulco. You're bullshitting."

"Fine, it was a hallway."

"Why waste time thinking about it? Adriana is cool because she's cool, and Gaby is crass because she's crass. There have always been cool moms with crass daughters and vice versa."

"I'm just trying to work out why I get along with the daughter while the mother pisses me off."

"Do you think it's because the daughter isn't sleeping with your dad?"

Mau looked Marta in the eyes, winked, and clucked his tongue. They burst out laughing, the cocktails and wines getting to them. The meat and mashed potatoes arrived, served in individual copper casseroles.

The pale-yellow mashed potatoes were inexplicably light and creamy. The consistency was different from anything Marta and Mau had tried, as though the potato had fused with the other ingredients. They were entirely smooth, without a single lump. The juicy, nicely marbled meat was so tender that you could cut it with a fork. Biting into it gave them the carnivorous sense of being at the top of the food chain.

They finished their meal and the bottle of wine. Marta asked for the check, but they brought it to Mau, and he paid it.

"Shall we get your shoes?" Marta said.

"No, thanks. It might be better to check out the Ferragamos. We have an entire week. Why get ahead of myself?"

"But you've been telling me how much you want them since we were in Mexico," Marta insisted. "Let's go! We have time. It's only two blocks away."

"I said no," Mau answered, noticeably irked.

"What's gotten into you?"

"I've made some heavy investments in the parking garages." In reality he'd been forced to pay off the union, which had threatened to file a labor suit against him. "I'm kind of short on dough until the fifteenth, when it'll all go on my card and I'll have more cash."

"Oh, silly, you should have told me sooner. Let's go. I'll buy them for you, okay? Let's go. You can pay me back later if you want."

Mau chose navy-blue moccasins with leather soles. They were the most beautiful objects he'd ever seen.

31
The Bed

Marta awoke. Her dreams had not been good. She couldn't remember anything specific. A whistling seemed to pierce her brain. Her tongue was as dry as a lizard's and tasted like cinder.

She'd wanted to be with Juan, but it was Luis who'd sat by her side, and she hadn't been able to shake him the whole night. She tried not saying a word and putting on her best bored look, but Luis kept talking her ear off and drinking to the point of slurring his words. Marta got up to dance and Juan followed her—he took her by the hand and led her to a dark corner. There, without a word, he kissed her in a way that sent shock waves along her spine. It unhinged something in her head.

"I've wanted to do this all night," he told her.

"So what stopped you?"

"I'm seeing Begoña," he said in her ear. "I thought you knew."

Marta wanted to slap him. Any other girl would have done it. Instead, she gazed into his eyes and kissed him strongly and tightly, sinking her tongue into his throat.

You never can relive a past night with the intensity of the moment; it's like a crime scene with blurry, inconclusive clues that need to be reconstructed.

Marta headed to the shower. The shower's steam made her feel faint. She wanted to erase the feeble memories from last night. She shampooed the smell of smoke from her limp hair, washed the traces of makeup off her face, and brushed her teeth. She got some air and water. Clean, weak, hydrated, and wrapped in a bath towel, she sought comfort in her mother's room.

The air was fresh and perfumed, the sheets lightly starched, the darkness complete. She slipped quietly between the sheets, just as she'd done a thousand times before, surrendering to the fluffy embrace of the goose-down pillows. She hugged her mom and tried to match her breathing, closed her eyes, trying to sleep a bit longer. Later, when her mother woke, she would open the windows, and they'd chat for a while.

Sunlight streamed through the window, illuminating the silk curtains before resting on the Persian rug. A maid walked in, balancing a silver tray with a French coffee press, whole grain toast, fresh-squeezed mandarin juice, and the newspaper.

"Would you like coffee?" asked her mom.

"Yes."

"Milk?"

"Yes."

Marti was sitting on the bed in a silk lace robe. She had thin, nearly transparent skin, violet eyes, and impossibly black eyelashes. Hers was a kind face that inspired respect and admiration. It was a face worthy of contemplation.

"How did it go yesterday?" Marti asked.

"Fine. I don't know, okay?" Marta said.

"You're very lucky. At your age I'd already been with your father for many years."

"But you loved him."

"Yes, I think I did. I don't believe I asked myself that very often."

"For me, sometimes the only thing that matters is that they love me. I want to see how many love me, and I don't ask myself if I like them or not."

"But you only need one," her mother said, turning to her with an affectionate look.

"I know," Marta said somewhat desperately. "There's no one who . . . You don't understand. You think it's great that we go out and that I can meet a lot of men, because they wouldn't let you do those things, and you have always been with Daddy. But it's not like I really get to know people. The music is deafening, everyone gets smashed."

"Marta!"

"Sorry, they get tipsy. Then Luis monopolized me all night. He was so plastered that he could barely speak. I didn't know how to get away."

"Next time, honey, just tell him that you have to go, and voilà. That's why you have a chauffeur. Wasn't he waiting for you outside? Or you go off to chat with your girlfriends, and that's that."

Marta didn't want to tell her mother that all the other girls had to get home by two thirty, the hour that separated the decent girls from the others. She didn't want to tell her mother that she had stayed behind to see Juan. Her mother lived on a different planet. She couldn't imagine that people drank until they fell on their faces, or that they took drugs, or that they only noticed her because she was blond and from a good family. Marta couldn't recall the last conversation she'd had with someone. Juan had kissed her, but he was Begoña's boyfriend. She'd already smoked a joint. Her cousin Raúl had offered her cocaine. The high school kids snorted Ritalin, and then there were the pills.

"Mommy, do you know what Ritalin is?"

"No, honey," said a distracted Marti, reading the newspaper.

Why couldn't she talk to her daughter? Really talk to her. Advise her to appreciate her freedom. Tell her that she should allow herself time to grow. Tell her not to take things so seriously before it was all gone. If she hadn't feared being socially ostracized, she would have told her daughter, Enjoy your sexuality while you can, before there are consequences. But Marti couldn't be certain just how much times had changed; she didn't want her daughter to develop a reputation. Better to remain quiet.

This bed, from which she had ejected her husband years ago, was testimony to all that she had not lived. Marti knew it and she lamented it. Not for a second did Marti fail to perceive everything she'd missed.

32

The Art Show

Little by little the gallery filled up with people. Larry made an effort to introduce Adriana to the important collectors. The more serious ones had visited the gallery beforehand to examine the works they would buy. Adriana did her best to seem calm and collected, but she felt a chasm between her inside and her outside. Inside, she was a nuclear atom ready to explode. On the outside, she spoke eloquently, answered unexpected questions, and hid her feelings.

"Is that your friend?" Larry asked Adriana.

Marta was everything Larry desired, a tender lamb for the hungry wolf. His mouth watered as he headed toward her. Adriana knew the routine: lavish praise on her; figure out what she wanted. He would offer her dinner, make her feel important, and then try to sell her not just one piece but two hundred. That was how art dealers dealt with clients. They were the ultimate predators among modern fauna. The wealthy were the gazelles of the savanna—first the government took a bite, then lawyers, followed by bankers, decorators, architects, and real estate agents, but no one got as big a chunk as art dealers. Who else could get away with selling a painted canvas for millions of dollars? Who else could have created this market from which she made her living?

Larry introduced himself to Marta and Mau, kissing her on the cheek and shaking his hand. Adriana greeted them as well. She wanted to thank Marta, compliment her on how good she looked, protect her from Larry, and get her out of there. But Larry leapt on Marta, and Adriana had to turn away. She couldn't protect Marta, and she preferred not to witness the bloodbath.

"So, you are Adriana's patron?" he said. "I was very pleased when she mentioned that you were backing her project."

Patron? Marta had never seen herself in that light. Her mother had been a collector, and she had daydreamed about it as well. Marta looked around. The canvases on the walls seemed immense. People gathered like ants, drinking and chatting.

Marta had modeled in charity events a few times. She liked the attention she got on the runway, walking with purpose, pushing her hips forward and her hair back while balancing on ridiculously high heels. She'd felt beautiful, yes, but not admired or respected the way people looked at Adriana. Marta wanted what Adriana had, and she wanted it now.

"I'm going to buy the most expensive piece Larry has," she told Mau when Larry went to greet another guest.

"What's that about?"

"I want him to know that I have worth, too."

"You're wrong," was all he managed to get out, noticing that Adriana was alone. "C'mon, let's go say hi to her. Maybe she can suggest a piece for you to buy."

Mau headed toward Adriana. Marta stood alone in the middle of the room. She was not going to let Adriana tell her what to buy. She would buy what she chose to buy. She felt a hand on her shoulder. It was Larry.

"Marta, I'd like to introduce you to Arthur Kauffman. He's a great friend of mine and an important collector."

"Arthur"—Larry turned to a tall, bald man—"this is Marta, a friend of our artist."

"No, no," Marta said, trying to correct him. She didn't want to be introduced as Adriana's friend. But the gallery was noisy, and it was hard to make yourself heard. "Do you want a drink?" was all she managed to blurt out. As she'd expected, Arthur rushed to get her a drink.

At long last they all left the gallery. Arthur was by Marta's side, talking about tequila. They ducked into a nearby dive. Marta felt more comfortable in familiar territory. Now everyone turned to look at her. She realized that her dress had crept up, and she didn't yank it down.

Larry had reserved a large table that dominated the back of the bar. Adriana, exhausted, sat on the banquette next to Mau. Marta started to turn toward them but then decided to ignore them. *Fuck 'em*, she thought, thinking her friends had abandoned her. Larry and Arthur sandwiched her on either side. They had ordered tequila shots for everyone.

"What's the matter with Marta?" Adriana asked Mau.

"What?" The music made it hard to hear.

"Why is she acting like that?"

"She's always been like that."

"What do you say we get some dinner? I'm starving."

Adriana took Mau's hand and led him out of the bar. He took one last look back at Marta, who seemed to be giving the old guy a lap dance. They walked a few blocks without knowing where they were heading and soon came upon a quiet restaurant. They ordered pasta.

"God, I haven't eaten well in three days. Thank you so much. I couldn't stand another second of that."

"It was a bit much."

"Has Marta really always been like this?"

"Yes, always."

"I thought—I don't know, I barely know her—but I thought, I don't know, I imagined her a different way."

"I think she did as well. I think we all did. But something came over her this afternoon. Hey, let's not talk about her. It's your opening, right? How do you feel?"

"Good. I'm tired but content. I think the show sold well, and I'm excited about the new project."

They finished their pasta and walked across town to Adriana's apartment. The evening was brisk.

They got to the building's entrance, and Adriana asked Mau if he wanted to come up.

"No, thanks. I'd better get back to the hotel and see what Marta is up to."

33
Death

Blood. Once again blood. Memories, ideas, feelings—she wasn't really sure what they were. Maybe air. Some nameless force, something abstract that came over her suddenly. Ghosts.

Had her feelings been fruit, Marti would've been able to classify every one of them—orange, banana, pineapple; frustration, anguish, sadness—but the moment she felt something it was as though she'd drunk a smoothie containing all of them. All her feelings mixed and mashed together. Surely a laboratory could identify the chemical changes in her blood. She was capable of feeling it all in an instant, even if it took hours to explain.

But now she didn't *feel* anything; she could only evoke the memory of the feeling, like a scar evokes the memory of pain. Bleeding no longer caused her anger or sadness, no longer made her run to bed crying. On the contrary, she knew perfectly well how to manage.

Even so the totality of her condition as a woman—centuries of collective history, the long path of the Y chromosome, and the years of her own personal history—could overtake her in an instant. She would think about ancient times, when they quarantined menstruating women. She recalled the cramps she suffered as an adolescent, the paralyzing pain and the fear. Then came the impotence of not being able to bear children: years obsessively anticipating the blood's arrival, counting the days, gauging her vaginal temperature, examining the stains on her underwear, and the devastating feeling of failure. It was nature's cruel joke, making the symptoms of menstruation and pregnancy so similar: the swollen breasts, the nauseated stomach, the lethargy. Even worse, she now believed she wouldn't make it to menopause, which she had looked forward to as liberating, when after a final cycle of hot flashes and ailments her hormones would cease to rule her life.

No, nature had another ace up her sleeve: cancer, her body's ability to obliterate itself. They were going back to Houston tomorrow. Marti knew she would never return from there. It didn't matter; she had put her affairs in order. She had protected and prepared Marta as much as possible. She could do no more.

It was not that she wanted to die. She didn't wish to die. The uncertainty, the not knowing, the nothingness—death frightened her; it frightened her deeply. But she was so tired of living. She felt constantly exhausted, her eyes closing of their own volition. She had pain in her joints and her throat. Her tongue was always dry, even after drinking, as though it were waterproof and rough, like a cat's. The loss of her beauty also caused her pain: her mutilated body, the scars. She feared death, but she did not want a life that she lacked the strength to enjoy or appreciate.

Inexplicably, or perhaps consequently, a part of her emerged and revealed itself in the face of her indifference toward life. At night she had the most vivid dreams she'd ever experienced. Perhaps it was for that reason that she didn't get much rest. Decades of insomnia seemed to unleash in deep dreams. When she woke, she had flown or been raped by multicolored dragons or eaten at banquets with Romans and solved the riddle of a scent labyrinth. She would wake with the sweet nectar of having nursed on the breast of a sphinx. Her clitoris pulsed recalling the erect, iridescent penis of the *alebrije*, that brightly colored wood animal figure from Oaxaca. From where did these dreams come? She'd never had them before. It was as though a tiny ember inside her grew into a bonfire every night and said, "There is life. This is life. Don't stop living." But that was *not* life; it was not the life she'd had. She decided that the ember had spoken to her from the other side, that she would live among dragons and fairies, indulging all that this life had not permitted.

34

Las Mañanitas

It took no time at all for Pedro and Marisol to get out of Mexico City. The metropolis, which seemed to go on forever, turned into pleasant green woods of Montezuma pines. They passed Tres Marías without stopping, and Pedro only had to slow down once, at La Pera, the infamous curve that took the lives of those who did not take it seriously.

Both of them were nervous. Despite knowing each other for four years, they'd never been so alone or so close. Four days stretched out in front of them like a distant star on the horizon. They'd always been on borrowed time. It was as though they had only crossed the river from one bank to the other, and now its entire length lay stretched out in front of them. They had stuck to a routine. Every Monday and Wednesday they would make love, go out to eat, take a stroll, maybe go to the movies, and then say their good-byes. Tonight they'd be able to sleep together the entire night. How many times had Pedro dreamed of this? Spending the night together and making love not once, but many, many times and then again in the morning.

They arrived at Cuernavaca, and Pedro drove to the hotel Las Mañanitas, where they would sleep the first night. Inside the sixteenth-century walls of red volcanic rock lay a harmonious and meticulously landscaped garden: bougainvillea and birds of paradise burst like fireworks. There were real birds, too—peacocks, macaws, flamingos, and cranes—walking about the grounds without trepidation.

"It's so pretty!" said Marisol, running up to a wall covered in *Monstera deliciosa*, enormous and exuberant leaves with holes and indentations. "They call these Adam's Ribs. I'm not really sure why; maybe because of the holes. They're one of my favorite leaves. Diego Rivera painted them frequently."

"Right," Pedro said, recalling a painting he'd seen in Marti's house. "And what's the name of those other flowers he painted?"

"Alcatraces, and these are royal palms. They're magnificent. See how the trunks are so smooth that they look like cement? And these, in the shape of fans that open so beautifully, are called traveler's palms. I don't know why they're called that. I've learned some of the names in Latin. Not that it's useful information, since no one else uses the Latin terms. You go to the plant nursery in Xochimilco, and it's like talking to them in Chinese. Pedro, thank you! What a pretty place."

They sat on cushioned chairs in the middle of the garden, taking in all the beauty. They ordered beer from the waiter, who left peanuts and potato chips on a small table of glass and steel. It got chilly once the sun went down, and they returned to their room. The fireplace was lit. It smelled of the local pine resin, an intense and pleasant odor that for Marisol triggered distant memories of starlit nights. It was a comforting and exciting aroma. She had on a wool sweater over a white cotton blouse and jeans. She pulled off her tan leather boots and put her feet by the fireplace. Pedro removed her socks and sweater. She shivered a little; he could discern the outline of her nipples. They kissed as if for the very first time. He grasped the nape of her neck with his hands, trying to contain her, to hold on to her entirety.

They undressed with casualness. She had to wiggle her hips to squeeze out of her jeans. He kept his underpants on, and they remained that way for a while, looking at the fire. Pedro was aroused looking at her. He loved her dark, smooth skin. She had large nipples, almost black, and her breasts were as juicy as mandarins. What he most liked about her was her ass: big and round like two papayas, and she had thighs like a pack mule.

"Lie on your belly," he said.

Marisol flipped over, leaned her elbows on the floor, and put her hands on her cheeks, gazing at the fireplace. Pedro started caressing her back. He went behind her and groped her like an animal in heat. He *was* an animal in heat, and he relished the friction it generated. He got hard in no time. He flipped her over and started touching her the way she had taught him. He kissed her breasts. He licked her earlobes, stroked her vagina with his fingers to warm her up, and when he felt that she was ready, when she was wet and panting, he flipped her on her belly and entered her from behind. He pounded her until she came, and when he finished he let himself drop on top of her.

"How I love you, *condenada*," he whispered as he kissed her neck.

After a bit he got up and sat by her side. Marisol lay on the wool rug, one hand supporting her chin, her gaze lost in the flames.

"What are we doing tomorrow?" she asked.

"Tomorrow? I don't know. We can have breakfast in the garden, swim a little, and do more of the same," said Pedro with a wink.

"You know I can't swim. I thought we could visit the nurseries at the Borda Gardens and Xochicalco. We should also go to Palacio de Cortés for the Diego murals."

"I'll take you wherever you like tomorrow, I swear. But today come to bed, because I'm exhausted."

Pedro brushed his teeth and put on his pressed white cotton pajamas. He slipped on his navy-blue leather slippers so as not to make direct contact with the floor. Marisol stayed up, watching the fire, until sleep overcame her on the rug. She got up a few hours later. The fire had gone out, and it was cold. Pedro was sleeping faceup, stretched out over the entire bed. She found a small spot and fell asleep snuggled in the corner.

They had breakfast in the garden. Marisol was impatient. She had gotten up early and gone for a walk. She enjoyed watching Cuernavaca come alive, the cobblestone streets and small-town pace so different from the city. When she got back, he was still sleeping. She had three cups of coffee on the terrace while waiting for him.

"What is it you so want to see in Xochicalco?" Pedro asked as he ate. "They say it's a pile of rocks."

"Rocks? Are you crazy? It was a city of twenty thousand inhabitants in the ninth century. Can you imagine? Twenty thousand! What's worse is that we still don't know much about it. How did they live? What did they think? A few marvelous structures remain, but since the Spaniards set themselves to destroying not only the people but the culture as well, all we have left are some clues. The observatory, where the sun aligns at midday on the equinox, remains extant. Can you imagine all they must have known? My archaeology friends told me I couldn't miss it."

It annoyed Pedro when she acted like an UNAM student. She had friends in every department—archaeology, biology, political science, literature, medicine—and among them they knew everything. Pedro didn't feel like driving just to see some ruins. He hadn't even brought appropriate footwear. But he couldn't say no to her. He knew they'd be on their way in five minutes.

They had a tacit agreement between them, one thing in exchange for another. I'll scratch your back if you scratch mine. They both knew they had to do it, and most of the time they fulfilled their obligations willingly.

It was the rainy season, so the landscape was entirely green. On the road to Acapulco they saw the turnoff and rode up a dirt track to a mesa. Pedro was annoyed. It bugged him when people spoke badly about the Spaniards. After all, he was Spanish. "Pedro de León," his mother would say, "is a conquistador's name." That always made him feel important. His hazel-green eyes and wavy blond hair were a point of family pride. In truth, his ancestors were not conquistadors. They'd left behind the hunger of rural Spain, emigrating at the beginning of the century in search of better fortunes. Marti's family, on the other hand, had been in Mexico for centuries. The Tordella de la Vegas even had viceregal palaces in the city center, which they had managed to conserve despite the War of Independence and the Revolution.

They got out of the car. The view from the mesa was impressive. Every shade of green imaginable and clear skies with puffy white clouds that seemed specifically designed for framing the landscape. Marisol walked about the ruins excitedly. She talked nonstop, explaining to Pedro everything she knew about the ball games, the glyphs, and the steles. Unlike Pedro, Marisol felt a connection to this ancestral culture. It was her history. The ancient pyramids were her home, the exterminated inhabitants her people.

"That's why I'll never feel complete. Octavio Paz got it right: we were screwed from the start. Our history is replete with abuse, submission, and rape. How can I attend Mass, pray to Jesus Christ, and follow a religion imposed by oppressors who destroyed my culture? Where can I worship Quetzalcóatl? We mistook our enemies for gods and screwed ourselves. I enjoyed the Concheros ritual dances in the *zócalo*, but that is not a religion. Besides, it's something they made up a few decades ago. Truth is, the fuckers managed to annihilate everything."

"Okay, enough, sweetie. We came to enjoy the ruins, right? Look, they're really impressive. Even I like them." Pedro neither understood nor cared about archaeology, but he had some sense when it came to real estate, and he knew that this property had great potential. The mesa overlooked the valley and was between Tenochtitlán and the coast, a perfect location for a business. No doubt these people—the Mayas or

Aztecs—knew the land well. "C'mon, let's go to the observatory. Don't get all worked up on me. What were the inhabitants called?"

A twelve-year-old boy guided them inside the observatory in exchange for a few coins. Pedro saw only a hole in the ceiling of a small cavern, while Marisol seemed to glimpse the very essence of the universe. Her head spun, imagining the stars in the sky and the complex mathematics that her ancestors used to precisely determine the movement of heavenly bodies.

"I don't know how to explain it to you," Marisol said to Pedro when they were heading back to the car. "I go through life without knowing who I am or what I should do, always acting on impulse. Then suddenly for an instant I can sometimes make out threads, the intricate workings, the entire fabric of my life, as though it all made sense. As though I had always been happy and knew what to do. Today in the observatory I felt that way. My whole life seemed clear—every knot, every stitch—and not just my life but existence itself. Has that ever happened to you?"

"No, never."

35

The Gringo

Marta woke in a king-size bed surrounded by silk-covered walls decorated with a collage by Matisse and a drawing by Degas. A chocolate-brown silk bathrobe hung next to the bed. She was still dressed in her clothes from last night, but she wrapped herself in the robe and sheathed her feet in the matching cashmere slippers that had been left on the rug.

Her head felt like a piñata after a party, but she was pleased to be in such a nice place. As flashbacks of vomit-covered floors and waking up in unfamiliar beds ran through her head, making the vein on her forehead bulge, she looked for signs of disorder. She had her underwear on. There was no vomit. She found her purse between some cushions embroidered with hunting scenes and confirmed that everything was there. Slowly, she pushed open the bedroom door.

She walked into a grand marble room with a spiral staircase that led to the floor above. A young woman dressed in a black uniform and a starched apron with white lace greeted her.

"Mr. Kauffman has gone to the office. He asked me to leave you breakfast and this note."

The woman motioned toward the bay window, where sunlight spilled onto a glass table on a gilded pedestal of carved wood. The sun shone directly on a bunch of grapes as large as plums and a parfait dish of wild strawberries with whipped cream. Marta watched the servant approach with a silver tray bearing steaming coffee and a basket of bread. She wanted to run away, but she restrained herself. She sat down, started eating, and opened the note:

> Dear Martha,
> It was enchanté meeting you. Hope to see more of you.
>   Su casa es mi casa. *La Grenouille* @ *8:30?*
>
> Yours,
> Arthur Kauffman
>
> PS Don't look for your shoes—you threw them out of
>   the cab.

She vaguely recalled tossing her shoes out of the taxi because they were bothering her. That old fucker—why hadn't he prevented her from throwing seven hundred dollars out the window?

Marta pulled some cigarettes from her purse and had a staring contest with the maid, which she won handily. Sparks flew in her mind. *"Su casa es mi casa"*—the asshole hadn't even gotten that right. Why the fuck had that phrase become the slogan of Mexico? *Whatever happened to "and let the cannon's blast shake the very core of the earth"?* brooded Marta as she quickly finished eating. *Mi casa es su casa. That's what we get for eating humble pie and lending our homes to others.*

Without saying good-bye, and still wearing the cashmere slippers, she left the robe on the chair and left. A doorman hailed her a taxi, and she headed for the hotel.

She reviewed her messages. Mau had called several times, worried about her. *How nice,* she thought. *Let him fuck off.* If he wanted to go off with Adriana, she wasn't about to get in his way. There were also three messages from her father. In the last one, desperate at not finding her, he explained that he wanted to start a business with Gaby. He was determined to come out ahead, but he needed a small loan—an advance, really—which he would pay back as soon as he'd closed the first few sales. Just a little nudge. At the end of the message, he begged her to help him. Marta did not return his calls.

36
The Mural

The next morning they headed out to Taxco. Pedro didn't want to learn about Hernán Cortés or listen to Marisol chatter nonstop about the conquistadors and how it would be more appropriate to call them colonizers, exploiters, genocidists, and thieves because to conquer suggests not only to defeat but also carries connotations of superiority. Marisol was so insistent on seeing the Palacio de Cortés, however, that Pedro dropped her off in front of the plaza while he went off to have coffee and read the sports section.

The mural's vivid colors seemed to breathe. They depicted a warrior dressed like an eagle, a suit of beak and feathers, the costume's cuffs adorned with lynx claws and, in one hand, a sling ready to be shot. *What a magnificent suit,* thought Marisol. Such a potent imagination: to think, dress, and desire oneself as an eagle. The Europeans, with their armor and rifles, bore the suits and weapons of cowards. In the background were flames. The plumed warrior was on the floor. On top of him a Spaniard protected by his shield and armor and mounted on a white horse brandishes his sword at an Indian dressed like fire, a barefoot fighter with only a mallet for a weapon. There is a jade bracelet on the floor. Marisol would have liked to pick up that bracelet, save it from destruction, and take care of it. She was ashamed of her desire. Had she, a survivor of massacres, been converted into a plunderer?

On a hill, Spaniards and Indians use their lances to fell an exuberant tree. Bodies hang from the collapsed tree's crown; they appear to be dead, but they support themselves. There are Indian bodies and Creole ones, too. Who are they? Why are they dressed? Do they represent modern Mexico? In the first panel the Spaniards fill their trunks with gold. Behind them, brutal violence: pain, oppression, weapons, forced submission. A braided whip and a spear frame the mural. Stone by stone the Indians are building the palace where she now stood.

Marisol took it all in as quickly as possible. She needed to hurry. The road to Taxco was still ahead, and she didn't want Pedro to get in a foul mood. She vowed to return to Cuernavaca in order to examine the mural in greater detail.

They didn't speak on the way to Taxco. Pedro was thinking that this would be his last night with Marisol. The following day he would be on a flight to New York. The trip had not turned out as he had hoped. He thought Marisol would be more interested in him. He couldn't forgive her for choosing a visit to the Palacio de Cortés over staying in bed with him.

Of course, she did not know this was the last time they'd see each other. He considered telling her about it, spilling the beans about getting married, starting work, being responsible, but he'd opted to keep quiet. He hadn't told her a single truth about his private life, so why start now? He'd told her that his father was an army doctor. The lies came easily to him whenever necessary.

Marisol watched the landscape through the car's window, the tropical greens intermixing with cacti and the pine-covered mountain they were climbing. She couldn't get the mural of the enslaved Indians out of her head. The Indians working in the cane fields and mines that created the area's wealth, the wealth of Mr. Borda, the exploiter. The images of October 2 and the Tlatelolco Massacre were engraved in her mind. Her memory was also burdened with recollections of friends who had disappeared. They hadn't been killed but were pursued by the authorities; they were in danger and had to flee to a province or hide in the sierra.

Next to her sat this man so white that he shone in the sunlight. He practically squeaked with his silver buckles, imported jeans, and fine moccasins. She felt simultaneously betrayed and betraying, victim and culprit. It had taken her four years to realize that Pedro used her as much, or more, as she did him.

The first year had been a dream: cars, restaurants, the occasional gift, and his steadfastness. Her friend Vanessa had to change boyfriends every week to obtain these things, and the rotation wore her out. The second year Marisol had renegotiated the terms. They had to bring Miguel along as well. They fucked once a week and went out twice. The third year she tried to ask for more: more money, more time, more information. He resisted. She resorted to other means and found out that he had another girlfriend, that his father was a businessman and not an army doctor. She followed him in a friend's car and staked out where he lived. The fourth year she went along with it out of inertia. She knew the limits of the relationship. She didn't expect more from Pedro, but she also didn't consider leaving him. She'd grown accustomed to him. He was part of her routine. She enjoyed his company and the *paseos* and couldn't find a good reason to break off with him.

Marisol didn't judge Pedro. He wasn't a bad person, just an ordinary one. He was caught in his own spider web. He was not going to help her. She'd have to weave her own shawl. She'd have to do it alone.

They arrived at the hotel and went for a walk. There was the pink stone of Santa Prisca, with its two bell towers and intricately worked facade. Marisol looked at it with interest. She imagined the Indians making the chubby cherubs, so alien from their own culture, and decorating the columns with vine leaves, which they'd never actually seen because the Spaniards forbade importing vines, olive trees, and even novels in order to maintain their hegemony. Then she imagined the columns worked with *Monsteras deliciosas* and rubber trees, as Diego Rivera might have sculpted them. Perhaps she didn't need to. The Europeans' project had failed. Santa Prisca was not, and never would be, a European cathedral: the souls that sculpted the facade had left their mark there, probably in spite of themselves.

They entered the church. Marisol headed for the Indians' chapel, the first Catholic chapel that the natives were allowed to enter. She tried to imagine the way people thought in that era. On the one hand, the Spaniards were obliged to convert the Indians to Catholicism. It took them a long time to determine whether the Indians were human, whether they had souls, which in turn would influence whether they were granted rights. When they determined that they were in fact human, it presented an enormous conflict in terms of justifying the appropriation of their lands. Even though the act had taken place many years earlier, there existed an a priori legal order, an established way of thinking. Some things could be done and others could not. The Spaniards wanted those lands. So how could they take them in a just manner? In the end it was Pope Alexander VI who decided that the lands could belong to the Spanish colonists—he was, after all, Rodrigo de Borja, born in Valencia—so long as they also took charge of converting the natives and thereby ensuring their place in heaven. The worst pope in history, so evil that he was later known as the antipope, finally conceived a way out that was tailored for the Spaniards. In exchange for their lands in this world, the Indians were guaranteed life in the next one. Otherwise, these infidels would be destined to spend eternity in hell without having known God.

Why hadn't they just left the Indians with their own gods? Marisol was enraged. She felt the hotel receptionist looking at her, as if to say, *If it weren't for the white guy you're with, the only way you'd get in here would be through the servants' entrance.* She felt the looks from the chambermaids and the waitresses, too. On the one hand, there was admiration, something like, *How did you manage it?* But it was immediately followed by disdain.

Pedro looked uninterestedly at the gold-covered altars. He liked the church, the smell of wax, the feeling of the cool, enclosed, shaded air. There were virgins everywhere: virgins and more virgins. He realized for the first time that the church was a cult of virgins. Not a cult of the Virgin but of virginity. Not the Mother of Christ for being his mother but for her intact vagina, because she'd never lain with a man. He imagined Marti's vagina: small, closed, pure. He thought about how he would penetrate her the first time, delicately and then forcefully, opening her and filling her. He'd never been with a virgin. She was to be for him only, his alone. By contrast, it disgusted him a little to imagine Marisol with another man's dick between her legs. Pedro knelt in front of the main altar and prayed an Ave María for his fiancée the virgin.

The restaurant was on a terrace facing the *zócalo*, the church's facade, and the red-tiled roofs of the town. Above these were spectacular clouds, fat and heavy with rain. The sun illuminated one of them, making it shine. The light outlined its shape and gave it a three-dimensional sense of volume. The clouds that were not lit up looked leaden, heavy, and threatening.

Marisol sat facing the church; Pedro faced the town and the mountain. Both were lost in their thoughts. They ordered enchiladas. They didn't speak. Marisol carelessly ate the corn chips and salsa they had brought to the table. Her crunching was audible. She chewed the fried chips with her mouth open. Pedro watched her. Suddenly, he didn't mind that he'd no longer be able to see her. What would he do with her in any case? In one year's time he'd have his proper wife in bed beside him. He could wait a year, but he'd have to take up running again. He decided to run a marathon.

They didn't even kiss that night. Marisol told Pedro that she wanted to stay a few more days in Taxco and Cuernavaca. She might as well visit

Tepoztlán, too, while she was here. She had some money saved from her wages and didn't mind taking the bus back. Pedro told her that he was going on a trip and would see her on his return. When he said good-bye, he gave her some money. He thought he spotted a shadow in her eyes that had not been there before. Perhaps she knew that they would not see each other again.

He got in his car and headed directly for the airport, just in time to catch the flight to New York, where he'd supposedly been staying the entire week. He had a day to carry out his mission.

The next morning he went to Tiffany's, as his mother had advised him to do, although she'd also told him not to miss Cartier, Harry Winston, and Forty-Seventh Street. He arrived at the store on Fifth Avenue. They took him to a special floor where they displayed only diamonds. Two hours later he emerged with the largest one he could afford. It weighed two karats. He paid in cash with the money his father had given him. Pedro hadn't been able to save enough on his own.

He presented it to Marti, as his parents had recommended, in a formal and boring dinner at the Tour d'Argent. Both of them felt completely out of place among the retirees and Japanese tourists. When they finished, they walked a bit along Saint-Germain. They needed to get back to the hotel in order to give their parents the news, so they didn't have a chance to see whether they would enjoy themselves simply walking along the street.

A year later they were married.

37

The Park

After parting ways with Adriana, Mau returned to the hotel and knocked on Marta's door, but she didn't answer. Back in his room he called her phone and her room every ten minutes until he fell asleep. When he woke, he tried to reach her again but still got no answer. He was used to Marta's disappearances. Sometimes a month would pass without hearing from her, but that had never happened while they were traveling together. He felt more responsible for and bothered by her than usual.

He left the hotel. He planned to walk along Fifth Avenue, but the park caught his attention, so he decided to go in. The leaves on some of the trees had started to turn; not that Mau knew the names of any of the trees. He wandered along the pedestrian walkways, passing a noisy carousel that played an instrumental version of "Ob-La-Di, Ob-La-Da." He came to an open field and saw a sign confirming that it was Sheep Meadow, where Adriana would shoot her photos. Mau crossed the path and bumped across a sculpture of a certain Mr. Webster. Was that the man from the dictionary? Mr. Webster's pedestal did not clear up the matter.

He headed north along a path. Soon he heard music. A solitary guitar accompanied an off-key voice singing "Imagine." He followed the melody until he came to a circular mosaic of black and white tiles. Smack in the middle was the word IMAGINE. Someone had placed flowers and rose petals along its edges.

He imagined a Marta who was composed, normal, and tranquil. A Marta he had always believed existed. How many times had he been told that she was not worth the trouble, that he should forget about that lunatic woman, only to keep trying? It was not like he had a choice. He was attracted to her like a superpowerful magnet, like the Acme magnets he saw as a child in the Road Runner cartoons. But he knew that he could never, ever express his feelings if he wanted to stay by her side. Marta had only two reactions to amorous advances: total rejection, or acceptance for a brief period, just long enough to split open the suitor's head and send him flying. Mau had no interest in that. His love for Marta was eternal. He wanted to watch her wake every morning, feel her naked back, and grow old with her. Imagine. Five years of imagining this and he had not tired of her, but he was growing weary of her impudent behavior. He had believed it was a thing of the past. She had seemed to recoup—until yesterday. It was already two in the afternoon.

His phone rang. He answered so fast that he didn't notice who was calling.

"Mau," said a voice that wasn't Marta's.

He felt relieved, let down, and curious. "Who is it?"

"It's me, Adriana."

"Hey, how are you? Have you heard anything from Marta?"

"No, I was going to ask you the same thing. Larry told me she went off with that guy Kauffman."

"Ah," said Mau, "exactly her type." Marta always ended up with rich, old, married men. Mau reasoned that these love affairs were displaced quests for her father, which would cease once Marta found her center.

"Where are you?" asked Adriana.

"In Strawberry Fields."

"Do you want to do something? Come over."

"Give me your address again. I'll grab a taxi."

"Take the subway. It's right there by the Dakota."

"The what?"

"The Dakota, where John Lennon lived, where they killed him."

"Oh," Mau said, having no idea what she meant.

"The subway is right there. Take the B, the orange line, at Seventy-Second and get off on Grand Street. I'll wait for you there."

They walked along Grand Street to Orchard and turned back along Rivington. The neighborhood seemed odd to Mau. It felt like Havana or Puerto Rico. Among the bodegas and old ladies seated on rocking chairs were modern stores brimming with character and restaurants with sophisticated fronts. They stopped at Teany, a tea café sunk a few steps below street level. The menu, handed to them by a waiter with a shaved head and arms covered in tattoos, listed hundreds of teas.

"This city is amazing. Did you know that there are white teas?" Adriana said, flipping through the pages that detailed countless varieties and surprising infusions.

Adriana ordered white tea and Mau had English Breakfast. They also ordered two scones, which came with a type of cream that was neither sweet nor tart. It was thick but melted in your mouth and tasted of cold milk. It paired perfectly with the scone's dry, crumbly texture.

Mau felt comfortable with Adriana. There was something natural and relaxed about her that put him at ease. He thought of himself as a trooper, a steady soldier who could stand firm during hours or weeks, but it was easier when he didn't feel that he was being evaluated or judged. With Adriana, Mau sensed the thin but perpetual layers of anguish begin to fade.

They devoured the scones. Since Marta was on both their minds, they avoided discussing her, exchanging opinions about the city instead.

It was as though each knew a different New York. Mau knew the stores, Adriana the museums, Mau the restaurants, and Adriana the streets.

"Come with me," Adriana said when they had finished their tea. "There's a store nearby that I've wanted to check out for days. I was going to take Marta . . ."

They went in, and Adriana broke off from Mau to check out one of the displays. It took him a minute to realize that the store sold vibrators. There were so many shapes and colors that it looked like a candy shop. One looked like a lipstick, others were small and portable. Some had innocent, childish designs, like a Hello Kitty head, but there were also realistic and even surrealistic ones that might have been designed by Salvador Dalí. There were sophisticated stainless-steel ones with accessories, and others that seemed discreet or humorous. They all had small signs with cursive lettering suggesting their possible uses. The store even had an entire section of waterproof vibrators.

Mau could not believe it. So this was what women did while they were getting ready to go out. Envisioning his female friends with a toy in the bathtub, he started getting aroused. He grabbed the one that was in front of him, a sort of five-speed submergible torpedo in bougainvillea pink.

"Do you want that one?" asked Adriana.

Mau hadn't noticed that she'd been watching him up close, nearly pushed up against his back. Lost in his daydream, he'd completely forgotten her.

"No," he laughed, instinctively checking the bulge pressing up against his jeans. "I already have one."

"I know," said Adriana. "But I thought since we're here just the same and since neither you nor I . . ." She wasn't sure what she was doing or what she intended to say or how to continue. "As friends."

"As friends," Mau repeated. He went to the cashier and bought the vibrator.

He could not make his legs move quickly enough for the three seemingly eternal blocks to Adriana's apartment. No sooner were they in the door than they rolled on the floor in an embrace, fighting to take off their clothes. The urge to be naked was stronger than any other. They did it in all three rooms and tried every position they could think of. Exhausted, they lay together, Adriana's head on Mau's shoulder.

"Would you like to?" asked Adriana.

Mau raised his right eyebrow.

"Do you want to leave the hotel and move in here? Why waste so much money?"

"As friends," Mau said mischievously.

"As friends."

It was already night when he arrived back at the hotel, well past checkout time. He had a message from Marta: *Dinner at La Grenouille. 8:00 p.m.* He threw on a suit and tie and ran out.

The restaurant's entrance overflowed with vases loaded with hydrangeas and carefully arranged branches. Mau caught sight of Marta seated on the main banquette. She was wearing a black sleeveless dress with a plunging neckline. She had on sunglasses even though it was evening. In front of her was the fat, bald man from the previous night. In an ice bucket next to the table, two bottles of champagne. Mau left without knowing if they'd seen him.

That very night he packed his suitcase. The next morning he checked out of the hotel and left a cryptic message for Marta. It was his turn to disappear. Imagine.

38

Insomnia

Used. She felt used. Like a gum wrapper—or worse, like a piece of gum that's been chewed up and spat out. She felt dog-eared and man-handled. They'd taken advantage of her. They'd seen her coming. She felt like the log that taco vendors use to chop meat on—the one that gets pounded with a hatchet until it's covered with dents. Did they love her? No.

Adriana had used her for money—Mau, too. He was always by her side, except when she'd needed him. At Adriana's exhibit, Marta had spotted them holding hands and leaving together. Since that time on the yacht when Adriana gave him a massage, Marta had known that Mau was interested in her, but she didn't say anything. Mau had used her to get close to Adriana, and just like that, he left.

How many times had her mother warned her? Every day of her life, Marta's mom had reminded her that one way or another everyone was after their money. Friendly overtures were just a ploy to eventually ask for something. "Don't let them take advantage of you," Marti would say. "Never discuss money. Stay with your social equals. Marry someone from the same class."

"Do you know what it's like not to trust the man with whom you share your life?" Marti had said once. "Money is power, Marta, that's all it is. The only thing it buys is power. A house, possessions—these are expressions of power. And power, my child, must be used wisely. It must be used for good. Understand? God granted us this power, and we have a responsibility."

God. Had God given it to them? Would God take it away if they didn't use it wisely? Were they some special divine breed in charge of distributing wealth? Surely, that's how her mother had seen it.

So, what would *she* do with that wealth? When Marta bought Adriana's painting, it lost all value. It just became one more object. She wished she could be like her mother and relate only to objects. They were less treacherous than people. What power did her wealth confer on her? She could buy whatever she desired. And? Time. She didn't have to work. She thought she was helping her friends, but look what happened when she tried to be good.

"Mommy, why don't I have brothers?"

"Honey, you know we could not. Rather, I could not."

"But I'm bored, Mommy."

"My love, did you know that I, too, never had brothers? Would you like me to buy you a pony?"

They never told Marta the truth. Every two or three years she'd ask the same question, and her mother always had a thoughtful answer at the ready. Because of *that question*, Marta had learned the art of horsemanship and gone camping; it's why they'd purchased the yacht and the house in Vail. Because of that question they'd eventually sent her away to boarding school in Switzerland. These palliatives worked for a while but never entirely eliminated her loneliness. Like a callus, some days it bothered her more than others.

For a long time anorexia was her close companion. Hunger both anesthetized her and kept her company. Above all else it had distracted her from other matters. Lacking nourishment, her body focused entirely on food. Now that she'd started eating again, she missed other things, a pile of things that could not be bought.

During these nights alone in New York, she drank in front of the television in her hotel room, sometimes watching porn, which disgusted and excited her at the same time. Eventually, she'd fall asleep.

One night her well-fed loneliness grew obese and began weighing heavily on her. She did not want to go up to her room. She drank martinis at the hotel bar on the thirty-fifth floor, with its views of the city extending out from the park. It was a cloudy night and only hazy lights were visible past the fog. A blond man with pockmarked skin approached her. In rough English he asked how much she charged. Marta guessed he was Russian. She didn't turn him down immediately. She thought about it but feared that she would not live up to his expectations. She gestured no with a slight movement of her head. After that it became harder and harder to sleep. The same ideas obsessed her. She was alone. She'd managed to scare away those who loved her. No, they'd never really loved her. No one. Never. Not even her mother had loved her. What should she do now?

The insomnia became unbearable. She called the hotel's doctor for a sleeping pill. The doctor was a young, attractive Filipino. Marta tried to seduce him, but he handed her a prescription and ran out. The pharmacy called the police when Marta refused to wait for her prescription. It finally dawned on her that she would be arrested if she continued behaving like a rabid dog. She stopped screaming, "Leave me alone, you fucking pigs!" and left with her head bowed.

When she got back to the hotel, she cried until her pillow was soaked. She could not remember the last time she'd done that.

39

The Honeymoon

Marti went to the bathroom to put on her silk lace camisole. She'd spent three months readying her trousseau. It was not enough to be a virgin on her honeymoon; she had to show up in new clothes, better than any she'd worn before. Everything right down to the last sock had to be brand new. She'd gone on three shopping trips with her mother and cousins, two to Houston and one to New York. Her friends admired her purchases: twenty camisoles in total, a different one for each night, folded in linen bags that were embroidered with her initials. Her suitcases, also brand new, were packed weeks before the wedding. She emerged from the bathroom looking pale, with a terry-cloth robe over another silk one and the camisole, which now seemed too thin. Her sweaty skin spilled out. Shivering, she slipped into bed without taking off her robes and pulled the sheets and blankets up to her ears.

"Are you sick?" asked Pedro, who was watching a soccer game on television.

"Yes. I think I'm catching something." Marti knew it was nerves, but she wasn't sure how to control them. Besides, she was exhausted.

The wedding had lasted twelve hours. She hadn't slept a wink on the plane. Now here she was with her love on her wedding night, and she wanted nothing more than to sleep and perhaps to be held.

"Rest," he said, fearing that she really was getting sick. "We have many days ahead of us." He turned off the light on the night table and asked whether she minded if he continued watching the game.

Marti, who longed for a hug and couldn't stand television, nodded and then pretended to sleep. Pedro lowered the volume.

The following night he tried to make love to her, but Marti burst out in tears and was inconsolable. The night after that they tried doing it with the lights off. He touched her and tried to seduce her, like he'd done with Marisol, but when he got on top with his stiff penis, Marti curled up like a piglet and remained in a fetal position until she fell asleep. Another evening Pedro suggested that she drink a little more than usual. That night she vomited.

During the day they visited sites recommended by the Michelin Guide. Marti took pictures and got excited seeing the Giottos, Rafaels, and Michelangelos. She tried to make the most of the trip. She made a game of picking out the Titians but would inevitably *si sbagliava*, as the Italians say. She'd been taught to identify Titians by the way he painted red velvet with exacting precision, but in the museum she realized that he was not the only one capable of such execution. Pedro feigned interest and followed along, staying out of the way. He knew that sooner or later it would be evening—not that it mattered, since she felt no passion for him. They were always together and they took care to hold hands, kiss on street corners, and ask passersby to take pictures of them. The fact that their honeymoon was a disaster remained their secret.

In Rome they went to the Vatican for an audience with Pope Paul VI, who gave them his blessing. It was to be a private audience, and Marti, following her mother's instructions, wore gloves and a black veil. In reality there were over fifty people dressed in every conceivable manner. Marti was disappointed. She had imagined being alone with the Holy Father and hoped that his presence would somehow solve their problems.

One afternoon Marti went shopping but asked Pedro not to come with her. She felt uncomfortable making him wait. She went into several stores on the Via Veneto. She bought a Valentino dress for her friend Sofía's wedding and a Gucci handbag, with its trademark red-and-green belt. She kept walking, letting the city guide her, and was soon in front of an American bookstore. She went in, looking for books about sex, turning nervously toward the door, fearful that someone would see her. What did she want to know? She couldn't explain it. She wanted to understand the sexual act. No one had explained it to her, and it wasn't as natural as she had imagined. What had she imagined? That it was like a kiss, but in pajamas. She hadn't even considered that it was done in the nude. She disliked having no clothes on and liked even less seeing her husband naked. She found several books that satisfied her curiosity. One, *How to Make Love like a Roman*, demonstrated various sexual positions. The photographs were not explicit, and Marti liked seeing the bodies interlaced, some with two or more men or women in finely furnished apartments. Feeling ashamed, she bought the book and hid it stealthily.

Locked in the privacy of her bathroom while pretending to get ready, Marti scanned the book—but not without praying first. Little by little she let herself be seduced by its images. She started kissing Pedro with more passion and began to feel aroused. Pedro also started touching her better, or so it seemed to her.

She came back from the honeymoon still intact, still a virgin, but they weren't sad. Every night they came a little further along, and at least the tears had stopped. Pedro had a bad case of blue balls. He was frustrated, but there was a part of him that was patient and confident. Patient in his belief that the moment would arrive, and confident that Marti would manage to overcome her inhibitions.

They returned home to a fully furnished house with two servants. It had three bedrooms, five bathrooms, a living room, a breakfast nook, and a dining room for twelve people. Marti insisted it was only their starter home and that she would get an upgrade once they had children.

Shortly after their return, Pedro started going out with his friends. Thursday was their day for golf and dominoes. One night they were planning a bachelor party for Eduardo, who would be marrying Sofía in a few months. Since Pedro was the first to get married, his friends asked him all sorts of questions. He avoided answering them, hoping that sooner or later they'd grow tired. He had nothing to say, so it was easy to remain silent and let his friends think that he was acting the role of a gentleman. A few years earlier, when he'd started his affair with Marisol, it had taken a huge effort to bite his tongue.

Marisol. He wondered how she was.

One night he came home smelling of cigars and Cuba Libres. Marti was asleep. Pedro put on his pajamas and lay down next to her, snuggling from behind. The booze, combined with being up against Marti's body—he couldn't contain himself. He started picturing a nice pair of juicy, round buns. He rubbed against her softly. His thinking fogged up as his erection grew. He couldn't keep his hands off her breasts. The same hands that pulled out his erect member tugged at his wife's camisole. Marti kept still and quiet, pretending to sleep. Pedro tried to proceed delicately. He pulled back his wife's panties. He didn't even remove them, just pulled them back a bit to make room. But there was no room, no way to enter her. He pushed against her with increased urgency and force, but she remained sealed. Aroused and furious, he removed her underwear and flipped Marti on her back. She kept her mouth closed and her eyes shut, turning her neck to avoid him. But there was no avoiding him. Pedro penetrated her with force. Marti bit her lip to hold back a painful scream. She was no longer a virgin. Pedro pounded her with force and anger until he finally came. He collapsed beside her and pretended to sleep as his wife's sobs grew louder.

The next day they behaved as if nothing had happened. From then on every Thursday night Pedro drank in order to get up his nerve and proceed in more or less the same fashion. In the end no matter how great the family name of Tordella de la Vega, Marti was his wife and had to fulfill her duties. Sooner or later it would cease to hurt her.

40

The Desert

Blood dripped down her inner legs. A nearly imperceptible pain had been her warning. Marti already knew what to do. Run. Run the bath and try to stop her heart with her hands so that it would not run away as well. Weep without making a sound. Remain completely still in that hidden nook, however long it took, until she could summon the courage to stand up, open the drawer, put on a thick sanitary napkin, and change pants. She would put on something black. She was in mourning. After two years trying to get pregnant, the diagnosis had been cautious but unequivocal. She was barren. She could not conceive. Or perhaps she could, but it would not attach to her uterus. Her body rejected it. They couldn't say why, even after the doctor had spent more time between her legs than her husband.

Dry as a desert. Infertile. She was sterile, incapable of reproducing. It hurt to see herself in that light. She felt it in her lungs; it poisoned her blood and corroded her from within. She, who had always been capable of anything.

Marti suspected divine punishment. She made multiple promises. It was the only way she knew to counteract divine will. She promised to never think about herself again, never feel superior to anyone, devote her life to children or mothers with problems, or even to both, pray every day of her life, recover her faith. She still had faith. So how was it possible that God had done this to her?

Impotence was horrible. She had never before felt vulnerable. From her earliest recollection she had asked for and demanded; she'd given orders, and they were followed. She'd wanted for nothing. They'd spoiled her as a child. They gave her sweets and gifts, they brought her breakfast in bed and put away her clothes. Now she had servants and a chauffeur. She bought, she managed, and she made decisions. Her mother, her father, the police officer, her friends, and in particular her husband always did what she wanted. But the only thing she wanted—what she most wanted—she could not have.

"Why keep trying if I can't have children?" Marti asked Pedro one night.

"The doctor hasn't said that," replied Pedro, rubbing her stomach. "He says to keep trying, that you never know."

"Yes," Marti said, holding back her tears. She was fed up with pity, with crying all day long.

41

Exhaustion

Every day Marti rose automatically and punctually at six in the morning. Once dressed, she read the newspaper and had coffee and toast with the television on. When Marta was a little girl, Marti always waited for her before having breakfast. She would only allow Marta to eat in front of the television or in the kitchen when she had work or social commitments and could not eat with her. When she was home, Marti would never leave her alone. It was sad enough that the girl didn't have any brothers.

But that was years ago. Once Marta began college, she no longer ate breakfast, and Marti no longer waited for her. Their relationship had been severed to such a degree that sitting down to eat was a huge effort, a hostile event that she preferred to avoid.

On this morning the fine drizzle seemed to float, as though the clouds rested on the floor like dew. The tree trunks were emerald green. A damp, velvety moss, more microbe than plant, covered everything. Her surroundings seeped into her bones, as though the nerve endings normally found in the epidermis had retracted and sunk to the depths of her bones, rooting the chill into the medulla and the marrow.

On her way to inspect the renovation of a center in the Doctores neighborhood, Marti could not recall a single time in her life when she had gone back to bed. But rest seemed to beckon her in this rain, and she'd asked the driver to take her home. The car made slow progress along Reforma. Marti automatically pulled out her agenda and started planning her week by jotting down notes:

Send flowers to Señora Del Valle. (She'd seen the obituary that morning.)

Order tickets for the festival at Centro Histórico.

Make New Year's reservations.

Pay the maintenance on the Villa del Mar house.

Have the waterproofing inspected.

Find a new driver for Marta.

Make an appointment with the dermatologist. (A few years back she'd had the spots on her hands removed with astounding results. It was time to do it again.)

She reread the list while they passed Petróleos Fountain, then recited the day's chores to Israel: florist, dry cleaner's, supermarket, pick up the suitcases that had been repaired. Israel never forgot anything. Yet he never did anything without being told. He would never have informed her, for example, that the suitcases he had taken in for repairs last week were now ready.

She didn't need to explain how she wanted the flower arrangement for Señora Del Valle. Ariel, the florist, had been designing Marti's arrangements for over ten years. But while scanning *Town & Country* at breakfast, she'd noticed a pyramid-shaped bouquet of white amaryllis with a banana leaf covering the bottom of the vase, and she liked it.

"Tell him to do it like this," Marti said, handing Israel the picture she'd cut out of the magazine. "If it doesn't look exactly the same to you, bring it to me, and I'll look it over." It was a blessing to have someone like Israel whom she could trust.

The driver honked, and the new gardener opened the gate. She had asked Pedro to order an automatic gate. It was the last bit of the entrance that had not been modernized.

She wondered if Pedro also felt tired. He used to diligently complete all his errands, as though he had resigned himself to do her bidding, and seemed happy to do everything she asked right away. But he seemed absentminded of late. The gate was proof of this.

Marti heard the maid's rubber soles approaching the vestibule. She carried a silver tray with a glass of water and her phone messages. Marti perceived the young woman's look of pity but didn't dare to ask if she'd had a bad night. She, too, had probably heard Marta come in at four in the morning and, like Marti, not slept well afterward.

42

Her Lips

There was a time when the image of Gaby's lips filled him completely. He didn't need to imagine anything else—only those full lips barely grazing him.

Pedro almost never kissed his wife on the mouth. Marti's lips were an abyss, a black hole. When his lips came into contact with hers, he lost all sense of desire, as if they were an electrical appliance that sucked up all his energy. His blood flow retreated, his hands grew cold, and his penis shrunk, as if he'd swum in icy waters.

His wife had asked him a third time to get the gate fixed. He didn't want to. He wasn't interested in obeying her orders or attending to her whims. The fact that they needed to better secure the property did not interest him in the least. Anyway, with a honk of the horn a boy came to open the gate. Why change that? The only thing he wanted to think about was being with Gaby, and with those lips. So full and soft, with that shiny gloss that smelled of strawberries. His pulse quickened, his desire swelled like a bullfrog's throat. His eyes shone when he thought of her. Marti's lips, on the other hand, were painted a bloodred that contrasted with her pale skin and violet eyes. They were sterile, just like her pussy, and capable only of rejecting, criticizing, and saying no. They were more likely to feel disgust than pleasure.

Pedro pictured Gaby and her small white teeth, her tongue provocatively licking an ice-cream cone. His memories of her were happy and erotic, pornographic even. Hers were insatiable, greedy lips that wanted to consume everything. Marti, on the other hand, would pick at a morsel in a three-star restaurant, her refined hand daintily holding the silver fork as she said, "Too much butter, don't you think?"

How had he put up with it all this time? Pedro wallowed in self-pity. He regretted having wasted so many years trying in vain to please her. He would not make the same mistake twice. He planned to enjoy what years he had left to live. He still had a few.

43
The Marriage

Almost without realizing it, they pushed each other away. They repelled each other like magnets of the same pole. He went to bed early; she went to bed late. He enjoyed sailing, and she got seasick. They maintained an active social life in order to avoid being alone together. They would stay married forever so long as each one kept to his or her respective side.

There were no conflicts, because they dreaded confrontation. They'd been raised to be pleasant; no one had bothered teaching them how to fight. They didn't know how to do it, not even to indulge in passive-aggressive behavior. On the contrary, they thoughtfully performed niceties. He folded back the bedspread; she brought him a glass of water. Marti bought him luxurious gifts, and Pedro lavishly feted her birthdays. These token gestures did not bring them closer. Each played their part in a carefully crafted script that did not leave room for interpretation, much less improvisation.

A few years into the marriage, Marti's father had spoken with her. He thought it would be best to name Pedro as his successor and executor of the family assets. "In reality he'll only collect the rent. For all intents and purposes Manuel will hold the reins. He has my full confidence."

Manuel was his right-hand man. No sooner had her father died than the right-hand man began amassing riches. She'd hear bits and pieces of information about how he owned the Bond ice-cream shops and a ranch in Oaxtepec. His kids were driving imported luxury cars.

Working up the courage to speak with Manuel took Marti several months. What else could she do? Ask for an outside audit? When she consulted Pedro about the matter, he naïvely remarked that he hadn't noticed anything, which only worried her more.

"What a surprise to see you around here," Manuel had said when Marti showed up unannounced at the office one day. "To what do I owe the honor?"

Marti had rehearsed her answer a thousand times over. She had goose bumps, but her voice did not betray her. "I'd like to see the account statements."

"All of them?"

"Yes. I'm considering a new venture."

"A business?" Manuel said, straightening his back and sitting up on the edge of his seat.

"No, more of a nonprofit foundation."

"I'll send everything to your home tomorrow. There are several boxes. Do you have someone to help you?"

"How silly of me! No, I don't," Marti said, laughing, "but I'll find someone. You know how stupid I can be." She laughed some more. "Have them sent to my house, please."

Ten banker's boxes crammed with papers were delivered to the house the following day. Marti was prepared. She planned to set up a maternity clinic as she had promised. Month after month Manuel deposited the same amount of money in her account, adjusted at times for interest or exchange rates. The funds fluctuated a bit depending upon the buildings, but Marti knew there was more to it. Using her charity projects as a ruse, she wanted to involve herself in the business and prevent Manuel and Pedro from deceiving her. That very day she hired a twenty-four-year-old business manager, a twenty-two-year-old accountant, and a nineteen-year-old secretary. Marti was thirty-two, her daughter already in preschool.

As soon as offices became vacant in the building where Pedro and Manuel worked, Marti took them over for her new project, dedicated to assisting pregnant women. Once she got started, no one could stop her. The needs of Mexican women had no limits and neither did Marti's drive. In three years she established three centers and a childcare facility. Marti threw herself into the work, passing by her father's old office almost every day and keeping an eye on the family assets.

44

The Business

Pedro hung up the phone. How was he going to tell Gaby that Marta didn't want to help him? She wouldn't even answer his calls! Gaby insisted that they set up their own business, but for that they needed money. They would have to rent a space, hire a secretary. How was he going to do all that? Without funds there was no way to move ahead.

He thought about all the money he'd spent on women. It was a small fortune—and for what? Had he saved that money, he could be supporting Gaby now. But no, he'd been a lecherous idiot, and this was his punishment. Pedro viewed his life as a series of bad choices—from beginning to end he'd made mistakes. Looking back, he saw that any other path would have been better than the one he'd taken. If only he hadn't married Marti. Now, almost sixty, all he had was Gaby. Even he realized that wasn't much.

He went to see her in the adjoining room, where she watched television while exercising on a treadmill. Avoiding her stare and her new boobs, he said, "She refused."

"Of course she refused," Gaby said, breathing heavily. She turned off the television and pushed a button to bring the treadmill to a halt. "What did you expect, Pedro? Did you really think she'd help you set up a business after throwing you out of the house? What planet do you live on?" She stared at him. "Listen, we don't need her. We'll start from scratch. Sylvia can lend us her office when we need it for meetings, but we'll make phone calls from the apartment. First thing tomorrow you're going to call all your buddies and tell them that I am starting a business, so it doesn't look like you need them, understand? Make it seem like it's something to keep me busy. If they know of a property, I can move, rent, sell, renovate, or manage it. Okay? We're in no position to put on airs."

"I don't have my address book," said Pedro, crestfallen.

"Then go by your office tomorrow and use those pretty eyes of yours to get it from the secretary. We are going to do this. Understand? Whatever it takes, we are going to do this."

"Fine."

"Here," Gaby said, handing him the newspaper's real estate section. "Help me by marking any listings that look interesting."

The following day, address book in hand, Pedro made calls. He considered talking first with the people he knew best, his cousins and close friends, but he felt a deep sense of shame. What if his voice gave him away? Would they think he was asking them for a favor? He decided to work in reverse, starting with distant friends. After spending an hour paralyzed in front of the table and in fear of being interrogated by Gaby, who was in the next room, he decided to begin with the letter *a*.

He dialed Javier Ábrego.

"Ábrego Industries Inc.," answered a voice.

"May I speak with Javier Ábrego, please?"

"Whom may I say is calling?"

"Pedro de León."

"From where?"

"What do you mean from where? From my house," said Pedro, confused.

Gaby leaned her head into the doorway and whispered, "Say it's a personal matter."

"What is this regarding?"

"It's a personal matter," said Pedro.

He was put through.

"Hello, Javier?"

"What's up, buddy? It's been a while! How have you been?"

"Good! You?" Pedro didn't know where to begin.

"Did you hear about Mario's son?"

"Yes, how awful."

"Haven't you read the paper? They've found him."

Pedro wanted to kick himself for not checking the headlines that morning. He'd been in such a rush to get in and out of his old office before the others got there that he'd forgotten altogether. "Yes, it's incredible," he said, hoping Javier would fill in the gaps.

"Unfortunately, he was found dead. They think it was the same gang as with Alberti's son, the ones who held the kid for two months. That time even after receiving the ransom they returned him half-crazed from torture. At least Mario can bury his boy in peace. Alberti is worse off with his son in the hospital. Can you believe it? Are you going to the service?"

Normally, Pedro wouldn't consider going, but it occurred to him that there would be a lot of people there, and it could be a good opportunity. "Yeah, buddy, I'll see you there. Listen, I wanted to chat with you about Gaby, my new wife. She's starting a real estate business, so if you know of anything."

"Of course, I'll let you know. I think my cousin Eugenio is selling his ranch in Tepeji. Call him. I'll put you through to Gloria so she can give you his contact details."

Pedro jotted down "Gloria" next to Javier's name, just as Gaby had instructed. Secretaries liked to be called by their names.

He went through the *a*'s and had at least ten leads to follow up on. He scheduled breakfasts, lunches, and a round of golf with Gonzalo Arteago. At three he sat down for lunch with Gaby and told her about his morning. Gaby took notes, and they divvied up the tasks and follow-ups.

"Gaby, my love," said Pedro excitedly, "I just realized something. I don't know why I didn't think of this before."

"What, Pedro, what?"

"The share in the country club!"

"What?"

"It's mine. The share is in my name. They don't allow women members. Gaby, it's worth almost three hundred thousand dollars!"

"But you're not going to sell it," said Gaby.

"Why not?"

"First, because we don't need to sell it. I told you that we're going to come out ahead. Don't you see? We already have over twenty leads. Some are bound to pan out. You're not even up to the letter *d*. Second, because you need it. Those golf outings are going to net you a lot of opportunities, my love. You need to have access. And third, because the first thing we would buy if we had the money would be that very same share in the country club, so there's no point in selling something you want to buy again. What we do need to do is put my name on it so that I can use the gym."

"What would I do without you?"

"And I you?" said Gaby tenderly, imagining herself in the gym with all those society ladies.

Three weeks later Pedro closed his first deal. The following week two more came through. They rented an office and hired a secretary.

They considered calling the agency "Gaby de León" but in the end decided upon using an English name, Lion and Lion. Its logo was a medallion with two lions standing up, their front paws raised like in the Exchequer Great Seal of England.

45

The Laboratory

He'd been married to Marti for nearly nine years and run fifteen marathons. Pedro felt like he was bursting, like his internal seams were ripping. After giving it a lot of thought, he decided to visit his cousin Rodrigo. With few words, because the last thing he wanted was to be indiscreet or expose himself in any way, he explained that if he had to jerk off one more time he was going to jump out the window. He needed sex, and Marti was not providing enough.

"You need a pro. Someone who won't interfere with your family life, who can't blackmail you, who doesn't even know your name," Rodrigo said. "Request a different girl each time. You won't be disappointed. When you feel the need, call them, and they'll set you up within the hour at a house in Las Lomas. The girls and the house change frequently. That's how they've kept up the business for over twenty years without a scandal."

Pedro jotted down the number on a piece of paper and began stuffing it into his wallet.

"No, dumb-ass, don't put it there. That's the first place they check. Why don't you memorize it to avoid problems? If they change numbers, I'll let you know. Oh, and don't be alarmed when you call them. I think they answer 'Medical Services.'"

Pedro tried to memorize the number, then stored the paper in his sock in case he forgot it. He'd forgotten to ask Rodrigo if he could call during the day. Marti kept close tabs on him even at the office, but it would be much harder for him to sneak out at night. He left feeling excited.

He went to the southern section of the city, where they'd just bought some buildings. The traffic moved surprisingly well, but on Avenida Universidad it came to a complete stop. That's when he saw a handwritten neon orange sign that said "Laboratorios Sol." He parked the car and stood outside the place on the ground floor of an apartment building. The windows were covered with black iron bars. She was standing behind the counter wearing a white lab coat. He stared at her for a while, unsure of what to do. When she looked up and noticed him, he had no choice but to go inside.

Feigning nonchalance, he said, "Is this your lab?"

"Yes, it is," she said, laughing. "I've been here three years and can barely pay the rent."

Slowly, Marisol came around the counter and stood beside him. She was a lot thinner.

"Don't be frightened," said Marisol, reading his thoughts as she gestured toward a wall of jars. "I'm not anemic—look, iron. It's one of the blood tests we run most often. Hepatitis, red blood cell counts. The problem is that people who have health insurance go to their network providers, and those who do not, don't pay. I'd like to do blood work for people with insurance, because their labs can't cope with the demand. But I need someone with influence for that."

The weight of her hand was the same. As was her scent. It seemed the most natural thing to him, as though ten years had not passed. She let him embrace her. Holding Marisol in his arms, Pedro felt strong and protective. He would buy her a real neon sign, send her warm food every day, and inquire among his friends for a contact with the Ministry of Health. After asking permission with his eyes, he kissed her. He had never needed it as much as now. Marisol stroked his hair.

"Wait a moment," she said, and went to shut the door.

She took his hand and led him to the basement, where among boxes, machines, and two microscopes, there was a small folding bed covered with the pink wool blanket from her old room. She sat on the bed, and Pedro rested his head between her legs like a child.

"How have you been?" she asked him. "I saw you married that girl, the one who was your girlfriend."

"How do know about that?"

"I always knew. Besides, it came out in all the papers."

He flushed, feeling momentarily ashamed. He felt like an arrow had pierced the shield of his lies. Marisol knew. How much more did she know? Yet she hadn't betrayed him. Pedro sat up and hugged her. He recalled the times they'd shared. He kissed her tenderly and removed her lab coat. He tried to hold back once he was inside her, but he couldn't.

"Sorry."

"Don't worry, I know you can last a lot longer."

Pedro wanted to make love to her again, but Marisol gently dissuaded him.

"It'd be better if you asked me out to eat someday."

He left feeling furious. He didn't even know how to screw anymore. He'd barely lasted a minute. What type of man had he become? He was no longer a man. As soon as he got to his office, he called Medical Services and set up a date.

46

The Pregnancy

Marisol sensed that she'd gotten pregnant while they were screwing. How had she fallen back into that old trap of the unhappy knight in shining armor? Why had she given herself over to supposedly comforting him? Hadn't she learned that he always used her? She'd been stupid, and she alone was to blame. She should've taken precautions; she'd even thought about it in the moment. She didn't stock condoms in the lab, but there was a pharmacy nearby. She was about to warn him not to come inside her, but he came so soon and, anyway, like an idiot she didn't want him to know that she wasn't sexually active. She wanted Pedro to think that she had lovers and that she was still attractive.

It pissed her off to care about the opinion of someone who shouldn't have mattered to her. It was a weakness that angered her. So did the fact that, despite her efforts, the lab was not successful. She could barely afford food for herself, let alone pay rent. She'd reached the end of her resources and her imagination. Her brother posted signs in most of the hospitals, and they both handed out pamphlets at bus stops every morning. She had visited over a hundred medical offices, and only three or four referred patients to her. The rest had implied that they wanted a commission, but she couldn't afford to pay commissions. She knew she should go back to them, tail between her legs, and ask for referrals, tell them that she would pay them somehow. And now this!

She didn't hesitate for a second. Her decision not to have the child was so visceral, so automatic, that it took her by surprise. She considered searching for her maternal instinct, to see if it even existed, but then thought better of it. *Best to leave it alone in case I should find it and start having doubts. Then I'd really be screwed,* she thought.

Having an abortion did not bother her. The embarrassing part was revealing that she was pregnant. It bothered her that others would find out how uncouth and weak she had been. Especially after the hard time Marisol gave Vanessa when she'd had to get an abortion three years ago.

She'd met Vanessa many years back when they both worked as hostesses. She found her crying in that stinking bathroom at the end of their shift. Some asshole had torn her stockings, and the owners were going to dock her pay. At the time Marisol didn't even know her name. But she kept a pair of stockings hidden in her bra because she was terrified that they wouldn't pay her. They'd already tried it once when a drop of ketchup had dripped on her uniform, but they'd let it go in exchange for a pinch on the ass. Marisol didn't really want to lend this stranger stockings, but Vanessa's sad look—plus her own fury at the thought that the bosses would come out ahead again—made her give them away.

Vanessa had paid her back immediately, and they'd been friends since, even though they had little in common outside the workplace. Marisol started dating Pedro, while Vanessa kept whoring around with no long-term prospects. Once Marisol was done with Pedro, she dedicated herself to the lab, but Vanessa remained her friend. She had an uncle who was a doctor, a mean bastard who had made her pay for the procedure even though she was his niece.

"I'm risking a jail sentence," he'd said by way of justification.

Marisol picked up the phone to call Vanessa. The sooner the better; she knew her friend could go days without checking in.

47
Sex

It drove her insane: his body's harmonious defined proportions, his toasted-bread aroma, the taste of his saliva, the coordinated dance of their tongues. Their capacity for pleasure was natural and automatic. They looked at each other, thought about each other, and their genitals immediately throbbed like those tiny lights on electronic devices that are always turned on. They left their names behind. They were no longer Adriana and Mauricio; they were "love," "baby," "honey," "sweetie," "good-looking," and "hot stuff." They called each other everything; they accepted any name because in the end their desire ruled everything.

Normal things stopped mattering. Whether it was hot or cold, indoors or outdoors, day or night, or whether the restaurant was good or bad, the only thing that mattered, and the only thing they could do, was to be together. They rushed to meet up, and as soon as they did they enjoyed themselves and became enraptured.

Adriana knew that it couldn't last forever. That knowledge enhanced her enjoyment even more. She remembered failed kisses where, after the initial desire, she wanted only to get away. She recalled teeth that scratched, tongues that shoved and gagged, and lovers who disappointed.

Mauricio had known his share of women: inhibited, demanding, screaming women who negotiated terms, who cried, repelled, accused, or were frigid and felt nothing at all. One woman had even confessed that she'd lost all sensation because the surgeon severed the nerves around her aureole when making incisions for her implants. Adriana was the exact opposite: pure sensation and enjoyment. He loved watching her delight, twisting with pleasure, moaning, and panting—she seemed to have no inhibitions.

They would snap pictures to make sure that the moment was real, that it wasn't a dream. Surrounded as they were by cameras and tripods, it seemed normal to record their intimate moments. They took care to make them artistic. Mau was a natural-born model. He could hold any expression without distorting his features. It surprised him how much he liked having his picture taken, how much he enjoyed being seen and then seeing himself later. He started taking pictures of her. He asked her to pose; he looked for her best angles, the curve of her hip, and the line of her jaw. Adriana's body was flawed, but Mau worked with shadows and body parts: her buns were hills, her white back a ski slope.

They spent the days in Central Park working on Adriana's project. Right away Mau fell naturally into the assistant's role. He scouted locations, looked for attractive families with children, asked them to pose, helped with the staging and lighting, and directed the other assistants. With Adriana's help, he soon learned how to use the equipment and began to get to know the work he wanted to create.

48
The Moon

Marta's hair started falling out. It was a while before she realized it. At first she dismissed the odd hair on her brush or in the drain of the hotel bathtub, but when it started coming out in tufts, she became alarmed. She suspected it might be a side effect of the sleeping pills.

She stopped taking the pills and started making healthy changes, like running in the park every morning. She had always been a good runner; it was time to get back to that. She also started smoking more in order to eat less. Then she checked out of the hotel room and rented an apartment at the Plaza Hotel. She didn't feel she could face going back to Mexico and her mother's empty home.

Recalling Mau and his promises, she resolved not to drink alone. Marta slipped into a backless Jil Sander dress and put on gold earrings, then fluffed her thinning hair into a back comb to give it more volume. Putting on makeup relaxed her—applying the foundation and blush to emphasize her cheekbones, curling and lengthening her eyelashes, outlining her lips for fullness. When she was done, she looked like a porcelain doll. Lace-up eight-inch heels in black patent leather, also Jil

Sander, completed the look. She called a car service and had the driver take her to Box.

It was immensely satisfying to watch a sea of people part in order to let her pass. Marta ignored the young woman who wanted to charge her admission. She had never paid to get into clubs, and she wasn't about to start. However, she tipped the coat-check hostess one hundred dollars to look after the white fox stole. It had been her mother's, and she did not want to lose it.

She felt tremendous relief upon entering the club. The music and first few drinks made her once again feel like the world spun on her axis. Why had she struggled with sleep when this was her true nature? Nightlife, noise, bodies pressing up against her—these things kept her from feeling alone. She pretended that Mau was waiting for her at one of the tables in the far end while she did whatever she pleased.

She met the gaze of a man who'd been staring at her and was soon sitting at a table with musicians who had pot and cigarettes. No one said anything about them smoking. They laid out a few lines of coke on the table and snorted it greedily. Marta felt completely renewed—dancing, enjoying herself, letting one of the men touch her under the table.

That morning, the previous night was a collection of memory gaps, but the overall sensation was ecstatic. Her head roared, but there was no chatter. Instead of internal dialogues, there was throbbing and a beeping that quieted everything. She took two aspirin. She tried untangling her hair but couldn't. In the process more of it fell out. She tied it in a ponytail and went for a run.

She slept late and went running when she woke. Then she shopped. She'd gotten to know some of the employees at Bergdorf, and it pleased Marta to be recognized upon entering the store. Afterward she'd take a nap or watch some television before going out dancing at midnight. She would rarely stay in watching movies.

One autumn evening Marta noticed the moon on a jog through Central Park. The days were getting shorter. She didn't know if the moon was waxing or waning, but she wanted to follow it, like the star that seemed to trace her steps after passing between the leaves. She thought about the Mexican moon. "México" means the place where the sun and moon come together. She thought about Ixchel, the Mayan goddess sometimes associated with the moon. She felt the force of the hate she carried inside.

Her stomach was burning up even while her legs marked the pace. Why had she been brought into this world? She cursed her father and all the men she had known. Marta even cursed Mau for having left her. He had always accepted her without judgment, right down to her seductions and madness, but no longer.

She watched the moon while she ran, wanting to unload the guilt she was carrying. Perhaps, she thought, she could reconcile with her father, but that was impossible while Gaby was in the picture. There was not enough room for both of them, just as there wasn't enough room for her and Adriana. She begged the moon to tell her what to do with her strength, her anger, her life. She kept running.

49

The Pictures

Mau used the camera to shoot Adriana while she slept. He went over her feet, her neck, and the curve of her back between the sheets. He turned on the computer and opened Photoshop.

Earlier that day they'd taken pictures of a Senegalese family, copying a work by Fra Angelico that they'd seen at the Metropolitan Museum of Art. Mau found the painting beautiful in its simplicity: Saint Joseph kneeling on the left with his hands raised in surprise; the naked Child resting on a blanket on the ground; and Mary, completely in profile, kneeling next to the Child with her hands in prayer. In the background was the geometric and primitive manger, like a Yucatecan hut, and the donkey and cow leaning in their heads.

Adriana had taken at least two hundred pictures in her attempt to recreate the image. Mau thought she'd erred in choosing a Senegalese family to represent such a classic, magical painting. He was interested in reproducing the painting with exactitude, whereas Adriana seemed to care more about framing a discourse on the possibilities of nativity scenes. Mau paid careful attention to the images on the screen, scrawling notes on his pad. He wanted to precisely recreate elements from the painting in order to put them all together later. He started with the Virgin. The Senegalese Virgin wore a white scarf on her head, snug jeans, and a fitted T-shirt that showed off her curves. Halfway through the photo shoot, Mau had recalled that Fra Angelico's Virgin did not have her head covered and asked the woman to remove her scarf. She obliged. Her hair was braided and pulled into a ponytail. Mau selected the pictures in which her hair was uncovered. The profile was an exact match because the original painting lacked dimension, and the Virgin appeared flat, as though made out of cardboard.

Adriana had not decided what to do about the golden halos that signified divinity in the paintings. She'd experimented with light, taking some test shots with the subjects' faces lit from behind, but these had not turned out well. Mau believed the photographs should have halos. He put Fra Angelico's painting on the screen and carefully cut out the golden rings. Then he manipulated them until they were the right size and pasted them behind the profile of the African woman. He enlarged the image and adjusted it pixel by pixel. When he felt the sun coming through the window, he turned off the computer and lay facedown next to Adriana, holding her.

Mau worked over many nights to achieve the desired effect, tirelessly repeating the same actions until he got the results he wanted. When he was done, he started another project. It was a photograph that imitated a Tintoretto nativity, for which he had directed the entire shoot. He'd set the child on a white sheet, making sure its drapes followed the original as closely as possible. He went days searching for a Saint Joseph who looked like the model in the painting—very old, bald, and with a beard. Despite the fact that New York parents were not generally young, Mau could not find anyone who looked the part. He felt defeated. Then he started searching for a grandfather. Adriana insisted that the families be authentic, real; he was not constrained by her rules.

One afternoon Mau was having coffee on a bench by the Literary Walk right next to Sheep Meadow. He was waiting for Adriana and hoping to hear a saxophonist who often performed there. It was his favorite section of Central Park; rows of large American oaks cast soothing shadows. He had seen pictures of these same oaks naked and covered with snow, and he longed to see them in winter. There were statues of writers placed under these trees, and for the first time in his life Mau felt a sting of curiosity toward their work. Why were they here? Suddenly, as though sent by God himself, there appeared a Saint Joseph identical to Tintoretto's, right down to the bald head and beard. Mau couldn't believe it. The man was pushing a toddler in a stroller; Tintoretto's Child was also big. Fortunately, almost none of the babies in the paintings were newborns. Adriana had photographed premature twins who were being taken for a stroll. They were barely as big as a large rat, and the photo turned out to be powerful. It was one of Adriana's favorites because it suggested the possibility of Jesus with a twin brother.

"Why not?" she'd said. "Even if the Holy Spirit fertilized her, she could have ovulated twice. Or the embryo could have divided itself after it was fertilized. Are we supposed to believe that God controls everything right down to the molecular level?"

Mau preferred to recreate the painting in all its beauty rather than ask himself those sorts of questions. The Tintoretto photograph on which he'd been working for almost a week was nearly identical to the original painting.

Mau had always dismissed photographs as souvenirs. For many years he refused to carry a camera because it bothered him that people would try to capture time in that way. You go up the Eiffel Tower: photo. You run with the bulls in Pamplona: photo. You go skiing: photo. Mau used to believe that taking pictures ruined memories. The trick was to be in the Eiffel Tower and not take a photo of it. Who cared about trite, touristy photos? The act of taking a photograph interfered with memory, because instead of living in the moment you were thinking about preserving it for posterity. It sacrificed the present for the sake of a future evocation. But now he felt capable of something altogether different. He didn't capture a moment with his camera; he captured an object. He created a new image that others could see, understand, and admire. What excited Mau was the possibility of creating images, because he'd spent his entire life looking without understanding why. Until now.

50

The Gallery Owner

It took Larry longer than he would have liked to organize the dinner for Marta. Adriana's show had sold out, and museums were expressing interest in exhibiting the pieces. He had not foreseen the work that would create.

On top of that, Adriana's and Mau's presence in the gallery distracted him. They used the conference room and computers almost every day. When they weren't shooting photos, Mauricio would set up in Larry's office, drink coffee, and look through his collection of monographs, devouring them as though he'd never opened a book in his life.

But Larry had not forgotten Marta. That would be impossible. She was like a wild colt, a magnificent animal that had never been tamed. You needed only to look at her magical eyes in order to understand that she took in the entire universe, that she was capable of anything because everything was possible with her.

He was pleased to discover that she was still in the city and decided to give the dinner that very week. It was customary to schedule events months ahead of time, especially during the busy pre-Christmas season, when the calendars of New York socialites were bursting with events. But Larry had devised a solution to this problem many years ago: Mondays. No one, no matter how in demand, had anything scheduled on Mondays, so Larry's dinners became legendary for the personalities he could bring together.

He invited several New York women around Marta's age to the dinner. Some were involved in charitable work, like Helena von Guttenberg, who headed up the Guggenheim Museum's Young Collectors Committee, or Paula di Gianni Mata, who had organized the benefit ball to save Venice. Larry could picture Marta taking a role as a global socialite, traveling from party to party on different continents. The girl did not seem ambitious, but he was confident that seeing other rich young women would trigger her competitive spirit, making her want to belong to that select group.

"Why are you giving her a dinner? Marta is not interested in art; she's not going to buy anything else from you," Adriana had warned Larry when he invited them.

Larry prided himself on having a great eye and an extraordinary sense of smell for sniffing out collectors. But Marta was not passionate about objects. She craved attention. Which is why he thought it would be good to involve her in the world of charity work. He'd witnessed more than one trust-fund kid morph into a social butterfly. Marta could be one of them. She just needed direction. Like Alejandra von Thurlow, a beauty with a tattoo on her neck who piloted her own plane and had been one of the pioneers of the organic-food movement. She also ran her own foundation and business. He was sure that Alejandra would enchant Marta.

Larry invited a few eligible bachelors as well. He didn't like that Marta had spent the night with Arthur Kauffman, even after he swore that nothing took place between them and that "the girl was fucking nuts." Kauffman was a hoarder and a glutton—in short, an authentic collector. In order to function he needed to acquire something every day: money, wine, women, or paintings. That was Arthur's day-to-day life. Marta could only fit into that life as a pretty and curious object. No, Marta was too valuable a specimen. Larry knew how to treat her right, how to protect her spirit and her freedom. A noble animal is delicate and needs to have its nature respected.

"Adriana, *querida*, I have a check for you. It's for your paintings, dear," Larry said excitedly. "They all sold. Now these photographs of yours, as you so rightly said, are going to be in great demand. I've already set aside the dates for your show next year, but I'll need the photographs within six months. They'll go to Venice, Basel, and London."

Adriana put the envelope in her backpack. She opened it only after leaving the gallery. One hundred and fifty thousand dollars.

51
The Check

Mau was sitting at the computer when Adriana walked into the apartment. He'd set out a candle, a bottle of wine, two glasses, place mats, and flatware on the round table, which barely had room for two people. He finished what he was doing and greeted her with a long kiss.

Mau couldn't cook, but every night he "made" her dinner with semiprepared foods that he put together or warmed up.

"Today I actually cooked," he said. "Well, I made mustard dressing because I didn't care for the ones I bought. I found a recipe on the Internet. Did you know there are thousands of recipes? I think I am going to start cooking for real."

Adriana welcomed the news. She wondered what Mau was up to all day on the computer and what he did besides assisting her. She couldn't deny that she enjoyed coming home to a set table, a flickering candle, flowers, and wine. Today, on the entrance hall table Mau had placed a velvety-red cockscomb. In the tiny kitchen, which was always immaculately clean, he'd prepared shrimp salad and country pâté on

French bread. Adriana worried that he would grow bored of not doing anything and leave her.

Whenever she asked him what he did, Mau offered vague answers. He lived on his earnings from a few parking garages in Mexico. He had majored in business but couldn't be bothered to finish his thesis. If he ever needed a degree, he'd buy it, but thus far not having one had not been an impediment. He once owned a bar in Zicatela, before that area became fashionable, and then sold it to a gringo surfer. He had properties, businesses, two married sisters, and seven nephews and nieces. His parents lived in a building that faced a golf course in Santa Fe, and they went to Acapulco every weekend. His father was a sailing aficionado. She had bits of information that didn't add up to a whole. Adriana saw a man who was handsome, strong, and serene, and who seemed to have nothing to do but give her pleasure. This seemed incredible to her. She worried that she'd wake one day to find the dream had evaporated. She sat at the table, opened the bottle, and poured herself a glass of wine.

"Would you like?" she asked Mau.

"Please. Hey, guess what I found out today?"

"What?"

"Remember how Marta told us that the farm animals were from the Central Park Zoo?"

"Yes, she knows one of the donors."

"Well, I got an e-mail from the caretaker, and they're from a farm on Long Island. Marta rented them."

"So Marta . . ."

"That's what I think . . ."

"Do you think that's why she's not talking to us?"

"I don't know," said Mau. "As far as I know, she doesn't know we're together. I think she's not talking to me because she's in one of her funks. The only thing that's changed is that in the past I would always go looking for her. But now, truth be told, you've kept me too entertained to think about her."

"Well, tomorrow is Larry's dinner, so we'll see her there."

Larry's check was burning a hole in her purse. She was no longer interested in Marta or her money. She took out the envelope.

"What's that?" asked Mau, sipping his wine.

"Let's toast," she replied.

Without asking what they were toasting, Mau clinked glasses with her. *"Salud!"*

"You're not going to believe it," said Adriana.

"What?"

"I'm rich."

"How?"

"Look, one hundred and fifty thousand dollars!" Adriana thought about what that meant. "I can stay here as long as I want and even rent a real studio."

They sat in silence. Mau imagined a financially independent Adriana with her own studio. Suddenly, it occurred to him that she might leave him one day. He hadn't thought about it until now. Their relationship was so natural that he'd assumed it was a done deal. It frightened him to imagine being alone again, returning to Mexico and not having anything to do.

"Why don't we buy an apartment together?" he said after considering all of this for a while. "I'll put up half. Here they let you finance up to ninety percent of the cost."

"I don't know. Wouldn't it be too much of a commitment? Like getting married?"

"No," replied Mau with a devilish grin, "because we wouldn't get married, but I have no intention of leaving you."

"Let me think about it." Adriana smiled. She was overwhelmed with happiness, but her instinct was to be cautious. There were too many emotions at once.

"I have something to show you, too," said Mau, heading toward the computer. "I was going to wait a few days, but with so much news I might as well share mine. I've been working on your photographs."

The Fra Angelico photo came up on-screen. Adriana was dumbfounded. It contained everything she had imagined and had not been able to capture. The editing work was a technical masterpiece.

"Mau! What have you done? How? How long did it take you?"

He just smiled. His eyes sparkled with an intense brightness.

Next he opened a photo that he'd conceived and directed himself, the Tintoretto. In terms of the characters, the Child, the Virgin, the draping of the garments and sheets, it was an exact and meticulous replica, but being a photograph set in Central Park, it looked modern and current. There was something of Gursky in it and Leibovitz, and something of Bill Viola. But it had something else, something nearly impossible to achieve: the artist's hand. Adriana recognized it at once.

"We'll sign this one together, but you're going to need to find your own project," she warned him.

"Don't worry. I already know what I'll work on next."

They dropped to the floor. The futon was a few yards away, but they made no effort to reach it. Mau removed her clothes, starting with her jeans. She unfastened the buttons of his shirt, revealing Mau's delicious pecs. Adriana's breasts were pale and vascular, her nipples dark, almost purple. Her pubic hair was black and luxuriant. Mau liked that; it reminded him of authentic, ancient women. Lush pubes signaled a certain maturity that inspired respect and admiration in him. Adriana had the body of a woman, not a girl; a woman who was open and enjoyed her sexuality.

Mau wanted an adjective to describe Adriana, much like "virile" could be used to describe a manly man. "Feminine," he knew, was the word he was searching for. But he associated femininity with something delicate, childish, and shameful, like shaved pubes and pink nails. Adriana was not like that. She was industrious, dominating, temperamental, sexual, voracious, lusty, and courageous. She was not afraid to live in the moment.

Mau pulled up her blouse and placed his head between his lover's breasts. He breathed in deeply. She smelled of sweat, dust, soap—she smelled of life.

He removed his pants. He was completely hard. She was ready, her legs open, her pelvis raised to take him inside her. He kissed her on the lips while penetrating her. Leaning on one hand, he tried to pinch her nipple with the other one and kiss her as he moved inside her. It was an uncomfortable position. He went in as deeply as he could and without warning grabbed her hips and flipped her on top of him. With his back on the floor, he could see all of her. Her tousled black hair, intense gaze, and bouncy breasts, which he alternated holding and squeezing. Lustfully, she leaned in toward him so he could suck and pull on her nipples, tickling her with his tongue. He grabbed her ass firmly. He wanted to photograph his handprints on her white skin. He heard her panting, felt her clamping him with her vaginal muscles, and he came as well, forcefully squeezing her ass.

"Get on the floor," he said, "like that."

He got the Nikon Reflex and put in a black-and-white 1000 ASA roll. He focused in tightly, so that her ass filled the frame like two full moons. His hands had left faint pink marks; the outlines of his fingers were still visible. The marks faded with each shot, and Mau doubted he would be able to capture the effect he wanted. Next time he would use the digital camera and more light. What was he thinking? He was no Mapplethorpe.

Adriana, still on the floor, looked on with interest, resting on one elbow.

"Leave that," she said. "I'm not finished with you yet. I want to come again."

Mau put aside the camera and smiled. When Adriana saw her lover's full lips spreading and noticed the twinkle in his eyes, she felt a pulsing just behind her belly button.

52

The Tub

Her throat was closing in. It was a struggle to free it, to free herself—she forced a cough. From the depths of her chest emerged copious phlegm that dropped into the clean water of the freshly filled tub. It was a huge and brilliantly white tub filled with warm, crystalline water, except for the floating phlegm that took on the shape of a snake trailed by bubbly foam. There was nothing else in that pure, clear water. Marta thought the tub could be its own universe. Fascinated and entertained by the gigantic phlegm, she decided to fill this watery universe with her bodily wastes, even her entrails if necessary.

She tried coughing again but nothing came out. She managed to pull out a few transparent snots from her nose, which though less thick in consistency were equally viscous and floated. She spat, but her small, colorless saliva did not alter the water's purity. She imagined opening her insides, taking out her organs one by one, intestines, stomach, kidneys, and all her viscera floating like planets in space. Her body was a universe. It had universal "potentiality." Why couldn't she pull it out without going to the extreme of gutting herself?

She conceived of a will where she demanded that the executor have her gutted, emptying out her viscera in a tub just like this one. She remembered a Goya drawing in which a group of cannibals quartered their enemies. "Let them exhibit me; let them make me stand out. I don't want to be buried in a coffin or burned." The bureaucratic impossibility of her request was apparent to her. It would be a crime to quarter her, even postmortem. The government would look after her body. "At least I can donate my organs." For a moment the image of her body divvied up, living in the bodies of strangers, filled her with happiness.

She started gnawing on her index finger. She pulled out a piece of skin and dropped it in the water. The tiny flap disappeared in the shadows between her legs. She kept gnawing until she drew blood and then dipped her finger in the water, hoping to dye it completely red. She wanted it to flow out of her in a crimson tide, like the wound of a lanced bull. But the blood ceased flowing almost immediately. The wound was not sufficiently deep.

She yanked at her hair. It came out easily and entwined around her fingers.

Disappointed and intact, she got out of the tub. She wrapped herself in a large, thick, white cotton towel and lit a joint before getting dressed. She knew she'd be late for Larry's dinner, but she needed to relax.

She wanted to cut her hair but found only cuticle scissors.

53
The Dinner

Mau put on a decadent forest-green wool plaid sports coat. It had red silk lapels with a small yellow-diamond pattern.

"The only things missing are velour slippers, a pipe, and a snifter of cognac," said Adriana. *Beauty and the beast,* she thought, looking at herself in the mirror while applying ChapStick. As always she wore no makeup.

"Will she know we're together?" Mau said nervously. It had been nearly three months since he last saw Marta.

"Yes. Definitely," Adriana said after thinking about it for a moment. "She's in touch with Larry. I'm sure he's said something about it."

Mau felt a little calmer. He didn't want a confrontation with Marta. Much to his surprise he hadn't missed her. Adriana and photography had filled his life in unexpected ways. He was afraid to hurt Marta, but more afraid that she would hurt them. He'd searched for her earlier that afternoon, hoping to talk, but she had checked out of the hotel. On the way back, passing Bergdorf Goodman he'd spotted the jacket and bought it.

Larry's apartment was on Seventy-Seventh Street in a building designed at the beginning of the twentieth century to house studios for artists. It had triple-height ceilings and an impressive view of the American Museum of Natural History. Since the apartment featured a wall of windows and the space was bright and open, Larry did not have any art out. That surprised Mau.

"What would a place like this go for?" he asked Adriana in a low voice.

"I don't have a clue. A lot. Although, knowing Larry, he bought it twenty years ago when it sold for a song."

Larry, dressed in a white silk Mao shirt, greeted them with a hug. "Come in, come in, I'll introduce you."

Alejandra von Thurlow wore brown velvet pants, Yves Saint Laurent ankle boots, and a gold sequined jacket. Her blond hair cascaded down in soft waves. Matteo, her husband, a Dutchman with cobalt-blue eyes and jet-black hair, was well over six feet tall and a sailing aficionado. By contrast, Paula di Gianni Mata was short, her hair pulled back in a tight ponytail, and she had black eyes and a husky voice. Adriana recognized Paula from the show and started chatting with her.

"Larry tells me you'll be showing in Venice. You must stay at my home," Paula said with a slight Italian accent. "I'll probably go to the Biennial, but even if I'm not there, there's always someone at the *palazzo*."

Adriana thanked her, knowing full well she wouldn't be staying there.

"Larry told me your nativity photos are very good. Did you know that my *gran-gran-gran-trisavolo* Cosimo was the man who commissioned Fra Angelico to paint the convent in Fiesole?"

Ah, of course, a Medici, thought Adriana.

"I'm interested in that photo."

"It's done if you'd like to see it. Mau helped me with it."

"Who is he?"

"Him," Adriana said, pointing to Mau, who was holding a champagne glass and discussing sailing with Matteo. She didn't know what to add, whether to say "my boyfriend" or "the artist." Until now she'd introduced him as a friend or even her "assistant," but she could no longer refer to him that way.

Little by little the other guests arrived. Larry had managed to get three prospects for Marta: Vincent Raddlefinger, heir to an old Swiss watch-making family; Claudio Montemayor, son of the Argentine ex–finance minister and owner of a chain of hotels; and Paulo Contatore, an Italo-Spaniard nephew of Berlusconi, who had made a fortune in real estate. Larry was proud of the turnout, but Marta had not yet arrived, and it was already nine thirty.

"Fuck, Larry, I know the guest of honor hasn't arrived, but I need to be in Dubai tomorrow. Do you mind if we start eating?" said a desperate Claudio.

"Not at all. It's late, so we might as well be seated."

In his twenty years as a gallery owner, this had only happened once before. That had been with Ana Mendieta, and only because she died. *She better be dead,* Larry thought.

Larry had planned a Mexican menu. Marta arrived a few minutes after the *huitlacoche* soup was served. Mau looked up. She was smoking, and her hair was all but gone; only a few blond strands covered her head. Her eyes, which she'd taken pains to make up, were sunken, as though her brain had sucked them in, and she was thinner than ever. Even so she was beautiful. She had on a black diamond bracelet adorned with skulls. Apart from that, Marta wore a fitted black leather dress and navy-blue Converse sneakers.

"Sorry I'm late. *Perdón*, Larry," she said, kissing his cheek and taking her place at the table. "You'll never believe what happened, the silliest thing. I could not find my shoes!" She put her sneakers on the table. "Only two days ago I bought the perfect pair for this dress: black leather Miu Miu platforms with a red rose on top. They were adorable, but I'm not sure where I put them. Ever since I moved into the apartment, I have such a fucking mess. The cleaning lady comes, of course, but she doesn't tidy up. Perhaps someone can recommend a good *nana*, Mexican-style, one who knows how to put things in their place."

Everyone stared at her, not knowing what to say.

Larry intervened, hoping to regain some of the normalcy that had reigned until that moment.

"Marta, allow me to introduce you. Well, you know Mau and Adriana."

Marta flashed a fake smile. Mau could not tell if she was joking or serious. While Larry introduced her to the others, Marta drank furiously and played with her cigarette. She looked totally anachronistic, like a silent-era movie star, with her pale face and corpse eyes.

She's a panther, thought Larry, *not a colt. A panther, a dangerous animal that cannot be kept in captivity. I made a mistake.*

Yawning without even covering her mouth, Marta stared at Vincent. "Vincent?" she said suddenly, pronouncing it in French as "Vansant."

"Oui?" he replied automatically, used to answering in five languages without giving it any thought.

"Do you remember me from Lausanne?"

Vincent looked at her as though seeing her for the first time. From the recesses of his memory, he called up the image of the girl she'd been fifteen years ago. He felt a knot in his throat that he tried to swallow down with a gulp of wine.

"What type of Mexican dinner doesn't have tequila?" Marta said in an inappropriately loud voice. "C'mon, get out a bottle."

"Marta," said Mau, wanting to make her see how out of place she'd been.

"What, dude? Like the good old days, right? Shots for everyone. Let's inject some fun into this party!"

She got up from the table and went into the kitchen. They could hear her opening and closing cabinet doors.

Mau looked at Adriana, who nodded in agreement.

"I'm sorry, Larry, I think she's not well. I'm going to take her home." Mau got up from the table and said his good-byes. "I'll see you later," he said to Adriana, giving her a quick peck on the mouth.

"Do you want me to come along?" she offered.

"No, it's better that you stay."

He went to the kitchen and grabbed her by the arm. He was angry, but he also knew that when Marta was like this, the only thing she responded to was force.

"Let's go."

"Where?" said Marta, as though they were going to move the party elsewhere.

"To your place, where else? So you can feel better."

A driver was waiting for them outside.

"To your place," Mau said.

"No!" she yelled. "Don't take me home—anywhere but there."

Mauricio insisted. The driver looked at them, confused.

"I am the one paying you. Take us to Box," said Marta, throwing her keys out the window.

"No," Mau said, looking the driver in the eye. "Don't you see she's not well?"

The driver nodded and drove toward Fifth Avenue.

"If anyone's not well, it's you," said Marta. "Since when do you kiss the help's daughter, huh? I saw you with Adriana. Have you sunk so low?"

Mau felt like telling her to shut up, but he didn't want to provoke her. The important thing was to calm her and make sure she got some sleep. Once they got to her place, he'd make her tea, and they'd settle in to watch a movie together. Sooner or later he had to calm her.

The car dropped them off at the Plaza Hotel. Mau went to the front desk and asked that they open the apartment.

"No, don't let him in!" Marta yelled at the doorman, sitting cross-legged on the floor.

Remaining calm, Mau approached the doorman and whispered, "Look at her. She's not well. I just want to take her up so she can rest. We don't have the keys."

"He wants to rape me! Call the cops!" Marta screamed.

The doorman didn't move. He'd never seen Mau before. On the other hand, the girl clearly needed help. Mau opened his wallet and handed over three twenty-dollar bills.

"All right, man, I'm trusting you."

The three of them took the elevator, and the concierge opened the door. Pile after pile of clothes, shoes, bags, and garbage were strewn across the floor, sofa, and table. The kitchen counter overflowed with shoeboxes and cigarette butts. The smell of stale sweat permeated the room, as though it had settled into the polyester fabric of her workout clothes, intensifying the effect with an acidic and penetrating note.

Marta cleared some room on the sofa; she sat there shaking and smoking, letting the ashes fall on the floor.

"What the fuck?" said Mau, picking up the clothes before realizing the futility.

"I don't have any booze because I no longer drink alone." Marta started to cry.

"You can't stay here," said Mau.

Mauricio held her gently, escorting her back downstairs and through the lobby. He was no longer worried that she'd try to escape. The bellhop hailed a taxi.

"What am I going to do with you?" asked Mau, looking her directly in the eyes.

"Toss me out like garbage," Marta answered in a girlish tone, staring out the cab window. After a long pause Marta, who had now become serious, said, "That's what I'd say to my mother when I was a girl. She'd hug me and say, 'How could I throw you in the garbage? You are my little treasure, the most beautiful thing in the world.' Well, I'm not beautiful anymore, so now you can toss me out."

"How can I toss you in the garbage," he said, holding her, "when you are my best friend?"

They walked up the narrow stairway to the fifth-floor apartment. Adriana was waiting for them, sitting at the dining room table. To keep busy, she'd pulled out a pencil and was drawing what she saw: the apartment door, covered in a thousand coats of paint, and its three locks; the bedroom door ajar and framing the futon, covered in a white comforter; the foyer table with the cockscomb and the mail.

"What's she doing here?" said Marta as soon as she walked in.

"I live here," answered Adriana.

"We live together," Mau said.

"Oh, I see, as roommates. Or are you lovers?" Marta cackled, collapsing onto a chair and lighting a cigarette. "Can you pour me a tequila? My blood sugar is low."

"No smoking in here," Adriana said.

Frightened, Mau turned to look at her, but he read Adriana's expression: *This is my house, and she is going to respect me. No one is going to start trouble in here.* Mau stayed quiet, waiting for Marta's reaction. She put out her cigarette on the table.

A few minutes passed. No one moved. No one said a thing. Finally, Mau headed for the bedroom and said, "I'm going to bring you some sweatpants and a T-shirt so you'll be more comfortable. Would you like some tea? We don't have a sofa, so I'll sleep on the floor tonight, and you two can crash on the futon. Okay?"

"No," said Adriana. "You two can share the futon; I prefer to sleep on the floor."

Marta got up and started looking around the apartment. She went over to the table by the entrance. She examined the desk and the computer. There was a metal shelf in the corner that held the cameras, tripods, a light box, and flashes. Marta sat on the floor by a large red cardboard box, where Adriana and Mau stored all the pictures they had taken. One by one she looked at the Polaroids, the contact sheets, the digital prints, the ones Mau had done in the darkroom, and the ones he had enlarged: Adriana's breasts like two moons; drops of water or sweat on someone's back; Mau, naked in black and white, posing like a Greek statue; Adriana's legs spread open, her genitals covered by an apple that had been bitten; Adriana's mouth as a flower vase; Adriana's ass like a flower vase; a hand pinching a nipple; Adriana in profile, lounging on the floor, splashed with red wine—hundreds of variations on the same theme. There was a particularly nice one of Mau's back covered with a handwritten poem.

Mau and Adriana watched in silence while Marta examined their bodies, their lives. When she was done, Marta went to the door and left.

"What should I do?" said Mau, looking for support from Adriana.

"Sleep; let's both sleep. Tomorrow you can call her father and see what they want to do. She can't go on like this."

"No, she can't," said Mau. "You wouldn't believe her place."

He went to the kitchen for a bottle of wine. A few drinks would help him to sleep. He should have gone after her. *I hope she went to bed,* he thought. *Why didn't I stop her?*

54

Fortune

Marti was about to leave for work when they told her that Lucy, the cleaning girl from Pedro's office, was in the kitchen, waiting for her. She instructed them to invite Lucy to the breakfast room and offer her coffee.

"It's a delicate matter," Lucy warned Marti.

Seated at the table with her hands folded on her lap, Lucy told Marti, after much beating around the bush, that the previous morning a young woman came to the office looking for Pedro. The woman was not a tenant or anyone she had ever seen before, so she became curious. Lucy explained, a little embarrassed, that she could overhear the conversation from the coffee station near the back of the office. She hadn't meant to eavesdrop, but she wasn't about to cover her ears either. She was in the middle of her cleaning routine, and they did not notice her. Lucy heard the woman say she was pregnant and tell the boss not to worry, that she had no intention of blackmailing him. She'd already decided not to have the child, but she needed money for the procedure. She knew a doctor who would take care of it. The woman told Pedro that she would never have come to him if she could manage it on her own, but she needed the money and, after all, it was his responsibility. Plus she thought Pedro had the right to know what happened to the embryo.

"Señora Marti, please forgive me, but I had to tell you. Your father, may he rest in peace, was more than a boss to us. Twenty years I've worked for your family. I prayed all night until the Virgin answered me. It's a living being, you know? I thought, *The Señora will know what to do*. You have a right to know, too." Lucy looked down at her folded hands, which were still in her lap, before adding, "I don't know if you are aware of this, but my sister Eusebia raised her seven children and five more that her husband brought home over the years. 'I can't help my lusty nature,' her husband would say, 'but I'm not going to abandon defenseless children.' She raised them as her own. My nephew Luis, who was your husband's driver, is one of those children."

"Thank you, Lucy," Marti said, making a mental note to send her a present the next day. "We're going to help out this girl, don't you worry."

Marti remained seated in the breakfast room until Pedro arrived. There was no time to lose. They needed to act immediately.

Marti was happy. God had given her an opportunity, and she knew how to act on it. He'd left the door ajar, and she had pushed it open. Wasn't life all about learning to recognize opportunities and knowing when to seize them?

Pedro clearly had no clue about these matters. But she had grown up watching her father make money. Every day when he came home for lunch, he'd discuss opportunities with her mother. Marti would hear about plans to open a train station and how it made sense to buy land nearby, or that they were about to build a road and it would be smart to invest in it. When she tried to discuss such matters with Pedro, he looked at her sheepishly.

"Why do you concern yourself with these things? I've put more than half of the money into dollars. That's why we pay experts, right?

Let the professionals take care of our money. You don't have to work anymore. Enjoy it."

Obviously, if she wanted something done she'd have to do it herself. Her husband had already gotten involved with this wench. It was up to her to rescue the child. *If I can save one life, my life will have meant something,* she thought.

Marti arrived at the charmless storefront on Avenida Universidad. She shut her eyes in disgust. Was this the sort of place her husband frequented? She bemoaned the fact that she didn't really know him after nine years of marriage. She had imagined him patronizing prostitutes in decent places, not lab assistants. No, in truth she hadn't imagined anything. She occasionally heard him masturbate, and from time to time he still pursued her. Marti was not naïve. She realized that their intimate life left much to be desired, but a laboratory on Avenida Universidad?

Walking in, she saw a dark, skinny woman with big eyes.

"Are you Marisol?" she asked.

"Yes."

"You're carrying my husband's baby," Marti said, looking directly at her, practically spitting out the words, as though she'd been chewing on them the whole way over and could no longer contain them in her mouth.

"What?"

Marisol hadn't recognized Marti at first, but now she did. The blood rushed to her temples. What did she want? Why was she here? Would she harm her? What should she do? She'd never expected Pedro to tell his wife. She thought he'd just give her the money. She'd wanted him to pay, to take some semblance of responsibility. Marisol hadn't yet answered when she realized that Marti de la Vega was crying. She took out an ivory linen handkerchief from a suede purse with gold buckles.

"I can't have children. Apparently, Pedro does not have the same problem. We weren't sure. In any case, Pedro told me you want an abortion. How could you?"

Marti looked at Marisol with such loathing and disgust that Marisol thought she might pass out. Her nausea, bad to begin with, tripled.

"I have not come to lecture you," Marti said, drying her tears. "I've come to tell you that you may not want the child, but I do. We were planning to adopt anyway. At least now the child will have my husband's blood. I am trusting in God that you are not lying." She placed a leather-bound checkbook and fountain pen on the counter. "Will two million pesos do?"

Marisol wondered how much the rings she was wearing had cost.

"That should be enough to start a business, don't you think?" Marti said, scanning the squalid room.

Marisol couldn't believe it: two million pesos. But what was this? Did they think they could just buy the baby? True, it was an unwanted child, and Marisol needed money in order to get rid of it. They were offering her money to give it away. No, they were asking her to sell it. *I will not sell my child,* she thought. But she didn't want it, and it really wasn't her "child." She'd told herself a thousand times over that she would be disposing of an *embryo*, a few cells that had mistakenly decided to multiply. This could be a good omen, one of those "things happen for a reason" moments. Pedro had arrived in his white Mercedes to save her from misery one last time. Marisol had gotten pregnant in order to give this woman the child she so badly wanted.

"I need to think about it," was all Marisol could say.

Marti did not want her to think about it. There was nothing to think about—she had to have that child; it was the right thing. This woman could not be allowed to kill it.

"Two and a half million."

"I'm not trying to negotiate," said Marisol.

"Neither am I. We can do this the easy way or the hard way. This country has laws, although some people might find that hard to believe. I've spoken to my lawyers. The life you have inside you is protected, and if you dare to harm my husband's child, I will personally see to it that you spend the rest of your days in prison. On the other hand, you could take these three million pesos and sign some papers tomorrow at this address. It will not be an adoption. In the eyes of the law and everyone else, this will be my child."

Marti handed Marisol the check. Three days later they signed the papers.

55

The Suitcase

Hunger gnawed away at Marta. Water. Water simulated the sensation of eating. There was nothing healthier than water. After the third glass, she felt like she'd throw up if she took another sip. It had happened before: foul-smelling water would come out, rancid water infused with her soul, her essence.

She considered eating an apple but would wait forty-four minutes before doing so. If she ate too much on one day, her body craved calories the next, and it took twice as much discipline to restrain herself. She liked feeling her body anticipate the apple's arrival. She had to make it last all day. It was easy in the morning, when she wasn't hungry, but after a workout her stomach roared, and she needed to force herself to eat only what she had set out. Sometimes she ate blueberries instead of the apple. In the afternoon she'd feel completely lethargic. Finally, at night, as though a switch had been turned on, she'd get a second wind and explore the parties and the people.

She lit a cigarette. People didn't get it. It wasn't about vanity. It wasn't that she wanted to be thin. It had to be this way. Marta did not need anything. The emptiness made her feel complete.

She spent a lot of time thinking about life. What to do. How to live. When to eat. She tried to quit smoking once more.

She bought four of the largest suitcases she could find and stuffed them with as many clothes as would fit. She dialed Adriana, as though nothing had happened between them, and made a date for coffee.

Marta was already there when Adriana arrived.

"I'm returning to Mexico," said Marta as soon as Adriana sat down. "I want to give you all my clothes. I really don't need them."

"You think that I do?"

"No. I'm asking you this as a favor in good faith. You can do whatever you want with them. The clothes are expensive. Sell them for all I care."

"You think I need your money? By the way, tell me how much it cost to rent the farm animals so that I can pay you. I don't need your help."

"No, Adriana, I did that for myself. I'm asking you this as a favor. I have to return to Mexico, and I don't know what to do with everything I bought. It would be stupid to throw it in the garbage, because it's valuable. That's all I'm saying. Look, if I behaved badly with you—no, let me rephrase that; I know I behaved badly. I want to apologize, okay? I need to take care of some things. I'm not sure what's going to happen. I wanted to give you these clothes. That's all."

"Fine."

"Take care of yourself, and take care of Mau for me. He is great, and I'm happy that you two found each other."

56

The Lottery

She put on a pair of jeans, the only ones that still fit her snugly, and some Ugg boots. She'd felt uncontrollably cold in her feet and hands, a chill that made her tremble and distracted her. She would have worn gloves if she didn't already feel like a freak.

She had prepared carefully for her return to Mexico and had every intention of doing it right. For once in her life she would do it all right. She was determined, no matter the cost. She'd gone two days without smoking. Fortunately, that automatically made her eat more. But she was careful not to eat junk. She carried almonds and dried cranberries in her purse. She started the day with an apple.

She put a relaxing playlist on her iPod and listened to it four or five times a day, as often as necessary. Inhale. Exhale. But she didn't plan to get hooked on it either. It was just a transition. Inhale. Exhale.

It had felt good to see Adriana again. Marta laughed, remembering that Adriana had been offended. She was so sensitive! In the end she'd taken the clothes, and that's what mattered. Marta wanted to travel with as little baggage as possible.

She did keep a black diamond skull bracelet as a reminder that death is always at hand, and a moon pendant that made her feel watched over and loved. It was a privilege to be a daughter of the moon, and she did not want to ever forget that. She also packed the stole that had belonged to her mother, her running clothes, two pairs of jeans, and some T-shirts.

She spent the last few days in New York walking the streets, even though it felt like being inside a freezer. The biting cold worked like anesthesia, which was exactly what she needed. When she couldn't take it any longer, she'd walk into a museum and pass the time. She had avoided museums because she believed they would remind her of her mother. She had only ever visited museums with Marti. But she no longer felt her mother's presence in museums any more strongly than on the street. Staring at paintings on walls made her forget herself for a while.

She visited the Frick and the Morgan Library. She enjoyed imagining their original owners. At the Morgan she broke her vow not to drink alone, ordering the champagne cocktail that the home's original owner used to serve.

She suddenly wanted a house of her own where she could serve cocktails to guests. She wouldn't have such a grand library, but maybe an impressive collection of movies and music. Nah, these days everything fit on a computer. What would her house be like? Why had she never imagined it?

Perhaps the fear of returning to her mother's house made her think of happier options. She could not stay in that house alone, flooded with memories. The last time she'd entered her mother's room she'd noticed, on the bookcase that normally had family photographs in silver frames, two wigs on faceless mannequin heads. One was light brown and styled in bangs, and the other was in a bun. They had used the third wig for the funeral, but its mannequin head remained there, eerily bald. She would take care of everything when she got home. She would sell it all, even the Diego Rivera.

What had her mother lived for? True, the maternity clinics helped hundreds of women every day, but what about the rest? *They should bury people with all their belongings like they used to,* thought Marta. *What do the living want with the possessions of the dead? Let them take it all with them; let them take it to the afterworld.*

Upon arriving in Mexico, she would spell out in her will that she was to be buried with her skull bracelet and pendant. She needed to leave detailed instructions for everything. Before, she'd imagined, perhaps stupidly, that Mau would take care of it. But now she would have to do it.

She boarded the plane with her earbuds in. The gum between her teeth kept her from breathing properly. She took it out and rubbed it between her index finger and thumb, as though it were Buddhist prayer beads.

She'd go to India to furnish her new home. She'd go to China and Vietnam to buy antiques. She'd use only the finest woods, certified as sustainably harvested, so as not to harm the forests. It would be a green house with solar panels and rainwater filtration. It would have a natural pool without chlorine, with lotus flowers to clean the bottom. Inhale. Exhale. She fell asleep imagining the house of her dreams.

She was the first to get through customs, because she only had a carry-on bag. Israel was waiting for her.

"Welcome," he said.

She'd have to fire him. Definitely. He reminded her too much of her mother.

The ride home was insufferable. Everything was the same as before. It was obvious that the maids had taken pains to attend to Marta as her mother had trained them. The Lalique vase in the dining room had white roses. They brought her telephone messages on a silver tray, along with a glass of water on a starched lace napkin. She ran up to her bedroom and locked the door. It was the only room in the entire house that belonged to her, the only room with smooth walls instead of wallpaper, and wood floors instead of carpeting.

Marta felt energized. She had slept the entire flight, but she didn't know what to do. She paced the room like a caged animal. She plunked down on the black leather sofa and turned on the television. "Sony Entertainment Television" came on the screen with that pseudo-seductive voice she knew so well. She turned it off immediately and, as if she feared its engrossing presence, unplugged it.

Her father had called her. He would have to wait. She didn't have any other messages.

She turned on her computer and went on Facebook; she had four hundred and fifty-three friends. What if she invited all of them to the house? Would they come? She could serve champagne cocktails. She'd throw a party like when she turned fifteen. It would be grand—pipe-and-hat style—à la Pierpont Morgan.

The thought cheered her up for a moment. Then she grew restless again.

She noticed the look of panic in the servants' eyes when she left the house wearing only shorts and a sports bra. Israel tried to follow her for three blocks. Despite wearing dress shoes, a jacket, and tie, he ran after her, warning her of the danger, telling her to at least put on a T-shirt and pants, begging her to return.

"You're fired," Marta finally said to him.

What was the worst thing that could happen to her? A bullet through the head? She'd be grateful. Rape? Kidnapping? She'd have to warn them that only she could pay her own ransom, and only if the trusteeship approved the payment.

She remembered Patty Hearst. Maybe she, too, could befriend the kidnappers and become a freedom fighter. She felt capable of planting bombs.

She came to the third section of the Chapultepec Woods, the part known as El Sope, and ran laps.

On the fifth lap a short, dark man started following her. Marta felt his steps behind her. She tried to keep a distance between them, but the man got closer. She didn't want to turn around or make him suspect anything. He was closing in on her. He came by her side. She instinctively checked her wrist; she had on her father's gold watch. She'd forgotten to take it off. Perhaps he was going to assault her. He kept running at her side.

"Have you run marathons?" he asked suddenly.

"No," she replied. Marta was intrigued. If the man was going to mug her, he wouldn't bother chatting. Or would he? Maybe he was a kidnapper.

"I can train you if you'd like."

"What?"

"I'm a trainer. I train people for the New York City Marathon. I take a group every year. We've been going for over ten years now. I trained Adriana Fernández. Do you know who she is?"

"No."

"She won the marathon in '99, when I trained her."

"Really?"

"Really."

They continued running in silence.

"You like running, right?"

"Yes," Marta said.

"I used to be a runner, but now I'm too old. Pardon me, but how old are you?"

"Twenty-six."

"You're at a good age. What's your best time?"

"What?"

"What's your best time?"

"I don't know. I've never run a race."

"Well, I can train you if you'd like. I'm here every day from six in the morning."

"I don't run in the mornings," said Marta.

"You'll need to get used to it. It's the best time. There's not as much smog. First thing in the morning you get up and run. You can have coffee and a banana, but the important thing is to start first thing in the morning. I don't recommend oranges, they're too acidic—a little toast is better."

"I don't get up early."

"Set your alarm," he said, before picking up his pace and leaving her behind.

She realized that he was checking his speed so as not to lose her entirely. She followed him. How could someone with such short legs run so fast? Marta watched his long strides. She ran as fast as she could as long as she could, her heart pounding. The man stopped, and Marta finally caught up with him.

"What's your name?" she asked with admiration.

"Federico."

"Marta," she introduced herself, putting out her hand and barely breathing.

That night she set the alarm clock.

Acknowledgments

Thank you to all who read this book and who share my passion for literature. I wish to thank my husband, Dave Morgan, and our daughters, Ana and Julia. My sisters, Jimena and Fernanda. My parents, Ernesto and Rocío. Eugenia Aguilar, Socorro Carrillo, Araceli Uraga, and Flor Romero, thank you. Diamela Eltit and all of the accomplices at NYU, Felipe Hernández, Alejandro Moreno, Renato Gómez, Rubén Sánchez, Margarita Almada, Carolina Gallegos-Anda, Javier Guerrero, Claudia Salazar, and Lina Meruane. Mario Bellatin for his transatlantic help. Thank you Sergio González Rodríguez, René Solís, Ricardo Ruiz, Inés Senillosa, Beatriz Blanca, and Miriam Morales for your readings. Thank you for your care, time, friendship, advice, faith, and company while I was writing *Becoming Marta*: Alejandro Rosso, Jessica Dayan, Diana Suárez, Andrés Ramírez, Florencia Molfino, Buzz Poole, Gabriella Becchina, and Ignacio Garza for his lovely desk. To all who were with me, thank you. The most special thanks to Gabriel Amor, who translated this difficult work, and whose talent and dedication shines through. He is the best friend and translator anyone can hope for. Thank you to James Fitzgerald, whom I met when I first came to New York and who had faith in me from the outset. And to my editor, Gabriella Page-Fort, who liked Marta and gave her this magical opportunity to become.

About the Author

Photo © 2012 by Arturo Zavala Haag

Lorea Canales is a lawyer, journalist, translator, and critically acclaimed novelist. One of the first Mexican women admitted to Georgetown Law, Canales worked in antitrust and electoral law in Washington, DC, and Mexico before joining the newspaper *Reforma* as a legal correspondent.

Since then, Canales has taught law at Instituto Tecnológico Autónomo de México, edited for the New York Times Syndicate in its Spanish news service, and worked for Felipe Calderón's presidential campaign in Mexico.

In 2010, Canales received a master's in creative writing from New York University. She published her novel *Apenas Marta* (*Becoming Marta*) in 2011 and *Los perros* (*The Dogs*) in 2013. Canales currently lives in New York.